The Reluctant Billionaire Bride

Roz Lee

ISBN-13: 978-0-9985706-9-3

DEDICATION

To the lucky lady whose experiences inspired this story.

.

ACKNOWLEDGMENTS

I owe a lot to many.
To my family for putting up with my habit of taking real life situations and twisting them to fit the story I want to tell.
To my readers for encouraging me to keep telling my stories. Without you I'm not sure I'd continue to torture myself.
To my editor, Laura Garland, for her dedication to getting it right and for her willingness to slog through the mess I send her in order to find the manuscript I *intended* to send.
To Talina Perkins at BookinitDesigns for the fabulous covers she creates based on the vague ideas I put forth.
I couldn't do it without any of you.
Roz

CHAPTER ONE

Julie stood in the shadowed doorway separating the workroom from the tasting room. The opening-night crowd swarmed around the bar, couples mostly, with a few singles mixed in. The locals she'd hired to be the face of Lucky Lady Brewing Company smiled at the patrons as they cashed in the free drink cards they'd handed out liberally all around Butte Plains for the last few weeks. In the half hour or so she'd been standing there, she'd seen at least a dozen customers return, paying for their next drink. "Who would have thought?" she mumbled.

A flash of light reflected off the vintage glass insert in the front door, illuminating her hiding spot and nearly blinding her. When her eyes adjusted, she crept forward again, scanning the faces for the newcomers. Scott Ramsey spied her first, waving an arm to get her attention. She waved back, letting him know she'd seen him.

"Quite the crowd," he said, joining her in the small alcove. "Congratulations."

"It's all your fault." A few months ago, she'd been content with the challenge of brewing craft beers. McKenna's Liquor took whatever bottled goods she sent over, never pushed for more than she could deliver, and didn't ask questions she didn't want to answer. It had been the perfect setup for a woman who valued her privacy as much as she did.

"I'll gladly take the blame," Scott said, eyeing the filled-to-capacity room, "but this is all you."

Julie shook her head. "All I did was provide a custom brew for your friend's wedding. You were the one who came up with the idea to open a tasting room." She'd been less than enthusiastic about the idea—until she'd seen the space he had in mind. Over a hundred years old, the structure had housed several businesses over the years but had retained its character. A sucker for vintage architecture, she'd fallen in love with the building. Perhaps it wasn't the wisest thing to base a business decision on, but if the opening-day crowd was an indication of things to come, it appeared to have worked out.

"Maybe." He shrugged. "But look at this place. You turned a pig into a purse."

Julie smiled. "Be careful. Your Yankee roots are showing."

"What?" The transplanted New Yorker feigned innocence.

"I made a silk purse from a sow's ear. If you're going to fit in around here, you're going to have to work on your vocabulary. Your money will only get you so far."

He dipped his chin, acknowledging her barb. "Words of wisdom I'll take to heart." The front door opened again, and they both turned to look. A trio of women—young enough they needed to be carded—walked in. Scott returned his attention to Julie. "Roseanne said you had something for us to sample?"

"Yep." Pushing through the saloon-style swinging door, she beckoned him to follow. "Come on. Your bride-to-be called earlier. She's going to be a little late. She had to go over to The Yellow Rose—something about a guest arriving without a reservation."

"I'm surprised Kay would need her help. Wonder what the problem is?"

"No idea. Not my problem." She stopped in front of a worktable holding six capped green bottles, sans labels. "Voila! My first attempt at nonalcoholic beer."

"These are for us?" Scott asked.

"I wouldn't do this for anyone else." She'd been working night and day on this brew ever since Scott and Roseanne had asked her to come up with something the pregnant bride could drink at their upcoming wedding. The challenge had been something she'd mostly enjoyed, but the time had come for a second opinion, and she was having doubts. She chewed on her bottom lip.

"I'm not making any guarantees. Could taste like rattlesnake piss for all I know." Not exactly true. She'd tried it and thought this version good enough to bottle a few samples, but you never knew what someone else might think.

Scott's phone belted out a synthetic version of Mendelsohn's "Wedding March." He held up his index finger. "Hold on a sec. I gotta take this."

"No problem." Julie leaned a hip against the worktable, crossed her arms, and studied her toes while her guest pressed the phone to his ear.

"Roseanne, honey. What's up? Uh-huh." Scott glanced at Julie. "Just showed up? You didn't know he was coming?"

Julie shrugged her shoulders, indicating she didn't have a clue what was going on, as she listened to the one-sided conversation.

"Okay. I'm sure Julie won't mind if I bring the bottles home." Holding Julie's gaze, he raised an eyebrow in question.

She shook her head. "Not a problem. I'll just box them up for you," she whispered then went in search of an empty box, leaving Scott to finish up his phone call with his fiancée. From past experience, she knew they usually ended their conversations with a bunch of mushy fake kisses and sappy endearments. It was enough to make a single woman with no prospects sick.

She certainly wasn't looking for a relationship. The microbrewery she'd started when she moved to Butte Plains was all the lover she needed. Sure, it made demands on her time, but that was as far as it went. She owned it, not the other way around, and as long as she stayed behind the scenes, she could reap the benefits of her little hobby brewery, and no one would connect Julie Davis with the person she'd been before her life went to Hell in a handbasket. And, it kept her busy. Gave her a reason to get up every morning.

She'd held various food industry jobs since she turned fifteen and got a job washing dishes at the restaurant across the street from the apartment building she'd grown up in. The extra income had been a welcome addition to their single-parent household, plus, her mother who was a waitress at the restaurant could keep an eye on her teenage daughter.

Dishwashing had led to waitressing then, when she'd turned twenty-one, she'd learned to tend bar. The extra tips she'd earned behind the bar helped pay her way at the local junior college where she'd received an associate's degree in business management. To celebrate completing her last exam, she'd purchased a lottery ticket and a full tank of gas on the way home. Handing over the cash for her purchases, she laughed with the cashier, a funny little man by the name of Marty, about all the things they'd do if they struck it rich. Never in her wildest dreams did she think she would actually win a lottery jackpot or believe the casual conversation could put her in danger. Her conversation with Marty Scruggs was one she almost didn't live to regret.

She'd all but forgotten about the lottery ticket she'd purchased and hung on the refrigerator door with a cheap magnet advertising a local auto repair shop. Her mother had seen it though, and while she'd dressed for her first day shift behind the bar, her mom checked the winning numbers.

For as long as she lived, she'd never forget the scream that brought her running from her room, her black uniform slacks forgotten on the floor as she hurried to do battle with whoever was murdering her mother.

She found her mom sitting at the tiny kitchenette table, her eyes filled with tears, her whole body shaking. Nearly incoherent, it took several minutes to understand what her mother was saying.

"You won!" she said. "You won!"

"I won what?"

Jan Harris waved a crumpled slip of paper in the air. She'd grabbed it, realizing what it was at the same time her mother engulfed her in a rib-crushing hug. "Oh, baby. You won!"

She'd extricated herself from the embrace and smoothed the slip of paper out on the table. "How many numbers did I get right?" She rarely played the lottery, allowing herself one two-dollar play a couple of times a year—usually on her birthday or when she'd passed a particularly difficult class. She'd won a few dollars once by matching three of the winning numbers. She'd cashed in the winning ticket and bought her and her mom both milkshakes at Sonic to celebrate the win. "I want a chocolate malt this time. How about you?"

"Hon, you can buy the whole damn drive-in! You won!"

Laughing, she'd stared at the ticket. How much had been up for grabs last night? Several hundred million, she recalled, but in truth, she hadn't paid much attention to the jackpot total when she'd purchased the ticket. Why would she? The odds of winning more than enough to add malted milk powder to a milkshake was roughly the same as reaching for the sky and coming up with a handful of stars. In other words—zilch.

"It says here there was only one winner for last night's drawing. Did you buy the ticket at the usual place?"

Her mom was breathless, but at least forming whole sentences now. She thought about the question. "The gas station on Travis Highway. I always stop there on my way home from school."

Mom held up her cell phone. On the screen was a photo of the self-service station she knew well. "Is this the place?"

"Yeah, but, Mom, hundreds of people, no, thousands, probably bought tickets there this week. That doesn't mean I won."

"The numbers, baby. Look at the numbers."

Willing to humor her mom but still excited to see if she'd won enough to maybe put a down payment on a new car, she said, "Read them off to me and I'll check them against the ticket."

Her mom read them slowly. She ticked each one off before moving on to the next. "Let me see," she said, reaching for the cell phone. "Are you sure those are last night's numbers?"

"Positive. See for yourself." Jan handed over the phone and began dancing around their small kitchen. "A billionaire! My daughter is a billionaire!"

"Mom." She'd laughed. "Stop being ridiculous!"

"I'm not being ridiculous. I'm celebrating. You're a billionaire!"

"I'm not..." The breath froze in her lungs. There on the screen was the date of the draw. She held the ticket up, found the same date printed beneath the numbers. The same numbers displayed on the screen. "There's got to be a mistake."

"No mistake, sweetheart! You won." Her mom sat down and reached for a pen from the Mason jar filled with writing implements they kept against the wall with the napkin holder and salt and pepper shakers. "Hurry up and sign it on the back, so no one can steal it and claim it's theirs."

She'd signed what had been her legal name at the time, Jennifer Harris, on the line marked with the X.

If she'd known the horror awaiting her because of that ticket, she would have stuffed it down the garbage disposal and said good riddance. But she hadn't. And she was Julie Davis now. A woman with no past and a lonely future ahead of her. Who said money couldn't buy happiness?

CHAPTER TWO

Could one kiss change a person's life?

Colin Parker knew the answer to the question was yes. If it was the right kind of kiss with the right kind of person.

He'd spent months trying to make sense of one kiss. Even went so far as to write a song about it. The song, and indirectly the kiss, had already changed his life almost beyond recognition.

Now, here he was back in Butte Plains to see if reality was as good as his memory, and to restore some sanity to his life. But first, he had to find a place to stay.

Colin leaned against the marble-topped island in the kitchen of The Yellow Rose Bed and Breakfast. His older sister's best friend, Roseanne Meadows, owned the place, and he was counting on her to let him hide out there for a few weeks. At least long enough for him to locate a permanent home for himself.

The thought of staying in his old room at his mother's house made his dick shrivel up, and there was no way he was going to beg a room from his sister. There wasn't a house big enough to accommodate a bachelor and a newlywed couple at the same time. He could only imagine the kind of things the average newlywed couple could get into, much less a couple who owned the hottest sex-toy business going. Imagining his sister being half of said couple was enough to make him break out in hives.

Having ruled out staying with his mother or his sister had left only one option. The Yellow Rose. He'd stayed here for a night or two for Becky's wedding, which had been held right here in Roseanne's garden. It wasn't the kind of place people would expect a single man to stay—which made it perfect.

"What's the problem, Roseanne? Why can't I stay here?"

"Kay told you why. We're booked solid for the next two weeks. Why don't you stay at your mom's...or with Becky and Ford? I know either one would be happy to have you."

He rolled his eyes. "Come on, Roseanne. You know why."

His sister's very pregnant best friend folded her arms over her gigantic belly and tapped the toe of one sandaled foot on the tiled floor while she thought his statement through. "Okay. I get it. A grown man might have issues staying with his mom. And Ford and Becky are still in the newlywed phase. Sometimes, I can hardly stand to be around them."

"Then you'll help me out?"

She let out a frustrated breath. "There really isn't room for you here. Kay wasn't exaggerating, we're booked up."

He opened his mouth to protest when she held up an index finger to silence him. "But, if you won't consider one of the new hotels out on the interstate—"

"You know I can't stay in one of those places."

"I suppose not. Which leaves one option."

Her grin made him rethink his decision to return home. "What?" he asked.

"My place. Well, it's mine *and* Scott's."

Roseanne and Scott had clearly put the cart before the horse, getting pregnant before deciding to marry. Becky had told him the two were living together now. "Seriously? How is that better than staying with Ford and Becky?"

"Our house is three times the size of Ford and Becky's. You'll have the entire third floor to yourself. Plus, if I'm cooking, there will be enough for you, too."

The promise of a steady diet of Roseanne's cooking made his mouth water in anticipation. She'd always been a good cook, and her recently published cookbook based on the recipes she served to her guests at The Yellow Rose had been on the bestseller list for over a month. Still, he should protest. It was the polite thing to do, and Heaven knew he'd been raised to be polite. "Are you sure? Shouldn't you ask Scott?"

"Scott will be thrilled to have another guy around, but don't think you have to hang out with him. Just knowing he's not the only Y chromosome in the house will make him feel better."

Colin huffed out a laugh, his lips curving into a smile. "It's a girl, isn't it?" He motioned toward her extended belly.

"Shh!" she said. "No one is supposed to know!"

Poor Scott. Outnumbered already. "My lips are sealed." He pushed away from the island and stretched his six-foot-two frame. His escape from Nashville had taken its toll. He needed a couple hours sleep and a beer. Not necessarily in that order. "Where is this house Scott bought for you?"

"You heard about it?"

"You know Becky can't keep a secret."

She led the way out the back door, through the neatly trimmed hedge separating the garden from the alley. "That's why I haven't told her the sex of the baby. She'd blab it all over the place and ruin the surprise."

He followed her around the corner and through a gate in a tall wooden fence. "Aren't you and Scott the ones who are supposed to be surprised?"

"Yes, but neither one of us likes surprises."

Colin was shaking his head at Roseanne's version of logic when she stopped in front of an enormous Victorian. His head swiveled, getting his bearings. "I thought this place would have fallen down by now."

"It almost did, but thanks to Scott, it's going to be here for another hundred years or so."

"Wow."

"I know. Impressive, isn't it?"

"Talk about an understatement." He took in the wide wraparound porch, the stained-glass windows he thought might be original, and the quirky paint job so typical of Victorian houses. "How big is this place?"

"Around five-thousand square feet. Six bedrooms and five bathrooms plus a library and two parlors."

"Holy cow!"

"Yeah, I know. I'll never be able to keep it clean, but Scott has an answer for everything."

"What's that?"

"Money. Hire someone, he says. Come on." She started up the walkway. "I'll get you a key to the front door. Take your pick of rooms on the third floor. I'd show you myself, but I can barely make it up to our room on the second floor these days."

"Not a problem," he said as he got his bearings in the newly renovated home. "How about I take care of the third floor while I'm here. I still remember how to make a bed."

18

"It's a deal." She handed him a key she'd taken from a drawer in the front parlor. "Make yourself at home. Help yourself to anything in the kitchen. We've got a grocery delivery service in Butte Plains now. Would you have ever thunk it?"

"Not in a million years," he said. "This place has changed since Ford came back to town." For the first time, he was beginning to question his decision to make this his permanent home. He wanted peace and quiet, not urban sprawl.

"It sure has, mostly for the good, though. Lucky Lady Brewing Company just opened a tasting room on Main Street. Grand opening is today."

An image of the owner of Lucky Lady burst into his brain like fireworks on the Fourth of July. Julie Davis. He'd met her at Becky's wedding then, later afterward, he'd seen her at a local music venue two of his high school friends had opened on the outskirts of town. They'd spent hours talking and listening to the amateur performers, some of which weren't half bad, before calling it a night. Well, actually, they'd been ushered out of the place in the wee hours of the morning. Waiting on the back porch of the B&B because he'd forgotten his key, he'd scared the crap out of Roseanne when she'd come down to start breakfast for her guests.

"You remember Julie Davis, don't you? You asked me about her the morning you almost scared me to death."

No way was he telling Roseanne how many times he'd thought of Julie since Becky's wedding. She'd run straight to his sister with the information, putting an end to any privacy in regards to his love life. Yeah, maybe coming home wasn't such a good idea after all.

"I remember her. Why?"

"She owns Lucky Lady Brewing Company."

"And?" She was fishing for information, only he wasn't going to take the bait.

"She provided the beer for the wedding."

Grateful for the opportunity to change the subject, Colin shrugged. "It was a beautiful wedding. You did a great job."

"Thanks. Kay wants to make weddings a regular thing we offer."

"You should."

Roseanne waved away the suggestion. "I don't know. It's a lot more work than it looks like it is."

"So, when are you and Scott tying the knot?"

"Soon. We're having a little affair here in a couple of months."

"Before the baby arrives, I hope?"

"It will be cutting it close, but yeah, that's the plan."

"If you need someone to sing, I'm your man."

"Thank you so much, Colin. Does this mean you'll still be here then?" That was the million-dollar question, wasn't it? "If not, I'll come back. It's the least I can do for you taking me in like this."

"Nonsense." A blush bloomed on her cheeks. "You're practically family. Our house is always open to you."

"Well, I'd better go get my truck." He added the key she'd given him to the keyring for his new truck. "Okay if I park in the drive?"

"Yep. Scott uses the bay on the left, so park on the right side."

"Thanks, Roseanne. I really do owe you one." He leaned down and kissed her on the cheek before heading out.

CHAPTER THREE

"Everything okay?" Julie set the six-pack of nonalcoholic beer on the worktable.

"Yeah. Seems we have an unexpected houseguest," Scott said, pulling the cardboard container toward him.

"I can't believe Roseanne would invite a perfect stranger into your home. Why not just send them down to one of the hotels on the interstate?"

"He's not a stranger. It's Colin Parker, Becky's brother."

It took a second for Julie to unlock her muscles. Everyone with ears knew Colin Parker. He'd been an up-and-coming country artist a year ago, but he'd recently had several songs hit the top of the charts and stay there. He'd become a household name, and one of the most eligible bachelors in Nashville. "Colin is staying at your house?"

"Apparently so. That's what Roseanne was calling to tell me. I think I'm supposed to keep it on the down-low, so don't mention it to anyone, okay?"

"My lips are sealed." *Bad choice of words*, she thought as memories of how her lips had parted for Colin's kiss. They'd just closed down a local music venue and been on their way to their respective cars, which turned out to be the only two left in the parking lot, and occupying adjacent lined spaces. The conversation they'd started hours ago inside continued as they sat on the hood of Colin's rental then, as the lights illuminating the parking lot winked out, revealing a sky growing lighter by the minute, he'd cupped her chin, turning her to face him.

He'd given her plenty of time to say no, but, looking into his blue eyes and seeing the man she'd come to know so well, she'd done the opposite of what she'd meant to do. She'd leaned in, offering up her lips for what had become in her mind as *The Kiss*.

Her toes had curled and heat had consumed her body as their lips and tongues dueled it out. He'd broken the connection. It sure as hell hadn't been her. She'd been too lost in the moment to think clearly. Thank God Colin hadn't been as affected. He'd gently ended the kiss then, being the gentleman he'd been raised to be, helped her into her car, and watched as she drove away. In the wrong direction.

She'd gone three blocks before she realized what she'd done and righted the situation. Embarrassed to be seen heading past the venue, she'd gone miles out of her way to get home. Yeah, she'd keep her lips sealed this time. There wasn't any reason to see Colin while he was in town. It wasn't like they were friends. She hadn't heard a word from him since he'd returned to Nashville. Granted, he didn't have her private number, she kept that unlisted, and changed it every few months, just to be on the safe side. Out of necessity, the brewery's phone number was available to the public, though. If he'd wanted to reach her, he could have done so.

Scott picked up his six-pack. "Guess I'd better be going. We'll let you know what we think of these."

"Thanks. I can bottle the remainder and slap on some labels in plenty of time for the wedding." She stopped herself from adding, "Tell Colin I said hello," before Scott exited out the back door, avoiding the crowd out front, but it was a close thing.

The last thing she needed was to see Colin Parker again. Just remembering the way he'd walked her to her car, without a word, and sent her on her way, should be enough to bring her to her senses. And if it wasn't, the fact he couldn't go anywhere these days without a bevy of fans and/or paparazzi following him should do the trick. The last thing she needed was to have her face splashed all over social media. The new life she'd worked so hard to build would come crashing down.

∾

He was taking a chance coming here, but as soon as Roseanne had mentioned Julie's new tasting room was having a grand opening celebration, he'd had to come. The place was interesting—a mix of old and new he could appreciate. He'd done some carpentry to pay the bills and knew quality work when he saw it. Half restoration and half modernization didn't come cheap, not if it was done right, and this had been done right. He couldn't recall a time when the corner building hadn't been vacant, which meant Julie had probably invested a small fortune in the renovation.

Colin made his way to the bar, expecting to find Julie there, her full lips smiling, making the customers feel at home. Not seeing her, he tilted his sunglasses down enough he could look over the top of them and scanned the room. The woman he'd come to see was nowhere in sight. Maybe she was working behind the scenes. A place like this had to have a storage room.

Politely edging his way up to the bar, he signaled one of the women serving foam-topped glasses of beer to the eager patrons stacked two deep.

"What can I get you?" the bartender asked.

Colin skimmed over the offerings listed on a blackboard behind the bar. "I'll have the…Don't Cry in My Beer?"

A smile broke on the woman's face. "It's a pale ale. You okay with that?"

"What would you recommend?"

"How about I bring you a sampler? Then, you can make an informed decision."

"Sounds like a good plan." He plunked a twenty-dollar bill on the counter. The barkeep swept it up, headed to the cash register. A few minutes later, she set his change down, along with a wooden plank on which six small glasses of beer sat in equally spaced cutouts.

"This one is Don't Cry in My Beer," she said, pointing to the glass on the far left. It was so pale, he figured he could read a book through it. "And that one"—she pointed to the dark brew on the far right—"is Stuck in the Mud."

"Looks strong."

"It'll grow hair," she said. "Looks like you still have all your hair, so how about trying the one in the middle? It's called Kissed at Sunrise. Better get it before it's gone. People are really liking it."

Kissed at Sunrise? The name reminded him of the last time he'd been in town. The sun hadn't exactly been up when he'd kissed Julie on the hood of his rental, but the heat from their lips touching had damn near burned him to a crisp. "I'll have one of those," he said, without even trying the sample. When she returned, he had to smile at the overflowing mug she placed on the bar in front of him. "Any chance Julie is around somewhere?" She had to be. This was the grand opening of her new tasting room. Who wouldn't want to be around for that?

"Julie?"

The barkeep brushed a long curl over her shoulder, revealing for the first time her name tag. Avery, it said. "Julie Davis. The woman who owns Lucky Lady Brewing Company."

"Oh, her!" Avery needed to keep her day job. An actress she was not. "Do you know her?"

"We've met," he said. "Would you mind checking to see if she's here?"

"Give me a minute." She held up an index finger. "I'll be right back."

❧❧

Julie counted the aluminum kegs stacked on industrial racks in the storage room. They'd been through a lot already but weren't in danger of running out. That would be a disaster! She was glad she'd opted for draught only beer in the tasting room. The commercial dishwasher she'd had installed could handle the glassware, as was evidenced by the volume today, but the bottling process for such enormous quantities would require her to add staff at the actual brewery, something she had no intention of doing.

Remaining a one-person operation limited her growth potential, but it was the way it had to be. She'd built the brewing room inside one of the barns on the old farm she'd purchased, which meant it was steps away from her home. After Scott Ramsey had come visiting, without an invitation, she'd had an electric gate installed at the end of the driveway, along with a surveillance system which allowed her to see and speak to anyone wanting access to the property.

It meant she had to stop what she was doing in order to let delivery trucks in and out, but having the peace of mind that came with controlling her environment, and her privacy, had allowed her to keep Lucky Lady Brewing Company in business. And, to expand.

She didn't need the money, but having grown up pinching pennies until they squealed, the idea of losing money, even when she had it to spare, made her physically ill. The brewery had repaid her initial investment, allowing her to pay for the renovations for the tasting room out of the profits. So far, so good, for a hobby she enjoyed, and kept her from becoming a total recluse. As long as she remained out of the public eye, she'd be a lucky, and safe, lady indeed.

A blast of sound from the tasting room had her looking up from her calculations. The woman she'd hired to manage the place, Avery Harper, closed the connecting door behind her. "Sorry to bother you, boss, but one of the customers is asking for you."

"Can you handle it, Avery? I trust your judgment."

"I appreciate your confidence in my abilities, but he's not asking for the owner, he's asking for you—Julie Davis."

Julie squared her shoulders. "Me?" Her heart raced. She'd been so careful to keep her face out of the media coverage the tasting room had generated. "What did you tell him?"

"I said I wasn't sure if you were still here." She placed a hand on the door handle. "Want me to tell him you left?"

Julie clenched her mechanical pencil with both hands. Lots of people knew her as Julie Davis. Nearly everyone in Butte Plains did. It could be a reporter from the local paper. They'd offered to do a short piece on the opening. Or it could be Randy Tucker, the contractor whose awesome renovations had made the tasting room a modern space, while retaining the historical character of the building. He'd promised to come by today. Still, she couldn't be too careful. "What does he look like?"

"Tall, dark, and handsome, though he's wearing a baseball cap and sunglasses. Inside."

"Cowboy boots and a button-down shirt?" She'd never seen Randy Tucker in anything but boots and dress shirt.

"Don't know about the boots, but he's wearing a T-shirt. Looks like he found it in a rag bin."

That didn't fit the description of anyone she knew. "I'll take a look on the security camera." She slid off the stool she'd been sitting on and headed to the small office Randy had built into one corner. It was both the manager's office and home to the expensive surveillance equipment she'd purchased. "Come point him out to me."

Avery stood over Julie's shoulder as the two women surveyed the crowd in the other room. "There," Avery said, pointing. "He's still at the bar."

Julie jerked her gaze to the monitor on the far right. Her breath caught. She supposed his choice of attire was his version of camouflage, but she'd recognize him anywhere. Colin Parker. What was he doing here?

"Do you know him?"

She nodded. "Yeah. I know him."

"Want me to get rid of him?"

"No. Just tell him I left for the day."

"Are you sure? He's kinda cute."

Too cute. Too well-known. If he got out of there without someone recognizing him, it would be a miracle. "I'm sure. As a matter of fact, you won't be lying to him. I am going home." She grabbed her purse off the shelf where she'd left it earlier. "Give me a few minutes head start before you go back out there. Okay?"

"Not a problem, boss."

"And stop calling me boss," Julie said, giving Avery a hug. "It makes me feel old."

CHAPTER FOUR

Avery disappeared through a door at the end of the bar. Colin took a sip of the foaming beer. His eyes lit with appreciation as his tongue swept over his lips to catch every drop of the cold brew. *Damn, that's good.* He took another sip, savoring the bittersweet flavor. The taste vaguely reminded him of a sunrise, full of promise with a hint of warning. Things could get really hot before the sun set again.

How many times had he thought about the kiss they'd shared? A million, it seemed. He'd even written a song about it. "Hello, Sunshine, Goodbye" had gone platinum a few months ago and rocketed his career to the stratosphere.

Watching the door for Julie wasn't doing any good. Watched pot and all that, so he spun around, taking in the packed room. His gaze touched briefly on every face. He was shocked to realize he didn't know a single one. It hadn't been very long ago he'd known everyone in Butte Plains, and they'd known him. Things really had changed in his hometown. Wondering if the growth was a good thing or bad, he shifted his gaze to the street outside the old but crystal-clear glass window.

A few people strolled by—strangers. Tourists? He'd heard Roseanne's fiancé, Scott Ramsey, had launched an advertising campaign designed to attract people out of Dallas to their little neck of the woods. It was an easy day trip by car from the Metroplex with plenty of things to do once you got here. Like have a brew at the new Lucky Lady Brewing Company tasting room followed by a stroll down Main Street to do a little shopping in the various antique stores and boutiques filling the once-empty storefronts.

Before Ford Adams returned to town and transformed the family business, Adams Manufacturing, into a successful sex toy conglomerate, Butte Plains had practically become a ghost town. It was just one of the reasons Colin had been chomping at the bit to get out of there. Since he'd decided to come home, he was a little disconcerted at the changes he saw. Where had the peace and quiet he'd once hated, but now craved, gone?

A flash of movement outside caught his attention. Everyone else was taking their sweet time, except for her. He caught a glimpse of the woman's profile as she turned her head to check for oncoming traffic. *Julie Davis.* Judging from the way she darted across the street, against the light, the minute there was a break in traffic—another thing Butte Plains didn't used to have—she was in a hell of a hurry.

Colin took another sip and contemplated the brewmaster's fine ass as she hustled in the direction of the new parking garage on Second Street.

He felt a tap on his shoulder. Turning, he smiled at Avery. "Not here?" he asked, knowing full well the woman in question had recognized him on the security camera mounted near the ceiling and hauled ass out of there to avoid seeing him.

"Sorry. I guess she went home. It's been a long day."

Tell me about it. "No problem. I'll catch her another time." He left Avery a generous tip—it wasn't her fault her boss got cold feet—and took one last sip of Kissed at Sunrise before heading to the pickup he'd left in the new parking garage a block over. Slipping into the driver's seat, he pushed the ignition button. A blast of cold air from the dash vent smacked him in the face. He chuckled at the irony. Slapped twice today. Once by Julie Davis. Once by the air conditioner.

Pulling carefully out into the traffic on Second Street, he mentally checked one thing off his "Reasons to return home" list. Reconnecting with Julie Davis wasn't going to happen. And here he'd thought that kiss had been pretty damn good. So good, it had sent him running back to Nashville.

A heavenly scent drew him through Roseanne's front door and straight to the kitchen. There were definitely advantages to bunking at her house instead of his sister's. Becky couldn't cook to save her life. Yet... "What are you doing here?"

Becky stepped away from the industrial quality stove, a wooden spoon in her hand. "I think that's my line." She brandished the spoon like a weapon. "Were you even going to tell me you were in town?"

Were all big sisters such a pain in the ass? "Yes, I was."

"When? On your way out of town? Does Mom even know you're here?"

He felt his cheeks turning red. "Not yet. I was going to see both of you tomorrow."

"Tomorrow." She wagged the spoon under his nose. "That's just great. I have to find out from my best friend my brother is in town, and oh, guess what? He's staying at *her* house, not mine!" Her anger seemed to evaporate. "Way to make me feel loved, little brother."

The sad expression on her face made him feel like the worst brother on the planet. How did she do that? "I'm sorry, sis. You know I'd stay with you and Ford, but face it, you just got married, and your house is kind of small." The only two bedrooms shared a common wall, and there was only one bathroom. Cozy for two, but not so much for three. They had gobs of money between them. Why they were still living in the old bungalow Becky had bought years ago was beyond him.

"You know you're always welcome."

"I know."

She smiled. "Just bustin' your chops, bro."

"You are the worst big sister in the world. I don't know why I love you." He crossed the room to place a kiss on her forehead.

"You love me because I'm the only person in the world who doesn't fawn all over you like you're some kind of celebrity."

The image of one sexy brewmaster came to mind. Apparently, Becky wasn't the only female who thought he wasn't the best thing on two legs. "You could be right. I can always count on you to keep me grounded."

"It's item number one in the big-sister manual."

He eyed the giant pot on the stove. "You aren't cooking, are you?"

Becky frowned. "No. Just minding the pot while Roseanne and Scott...well, whatever they're doing is none of my business."

Colin held both hands up, palms out. "Please, spare me that image! I've got to be under the same roof with these people."

"You have options. Don't pretend you don't."

He held up one finger. "Your house. Which we've determined is not an option." A second finger went up. "Mom's house." He frowned. "Think about that for a while."

Becky made a silly face. "Okay. I can see how it might be awkward for you."

"And last." A third finger joined the other two. "One of those cheap hotels out on the interstate. I don't want to toot my own horn, but get real, sis. Even I'm entitled to a little privacy now and then."

"Scott will kick you out on your ass if he finds paparazzi on his porch."

"I know, and I'll be careful. With a little luck, I'll be out of here soon."

"What do you mean? You just got here."

"I mean out of their house and their hair." He paused for dramatic effect. "I've decided to move back to Butte Plains."

"Oh. My. God!" Becky launched herself at him, hugging him tight while her feet danced a jig. To be on the safe side, he moved his toes out of reach. "I can't believe it!"

He carefully extricated himself from her embrace. "I've got to find a place to live. I want some acreage. Maybe an old house I can fix up. A barn I can convert to a recording studio. And privacy. That's my number one requirement."

"Wow. You've given this some thought, haven't you?"

"Yeah. I've been thinking about it for a while. With the local airport up and running again, I can commute to Nashville when I need to, or anywhere else I need to go. Most of my work is done at home or in the recording studio anyway."

"Don't forget touring." Becky adjusted the flame under the cook pot then resumed stirring the contents.

"I haven't. But it would sure be nice to have a place to come home to. I hate my apartment in Nashville."

"Do you have a place in mind?"

He shook his head. "No. There are a couple of old farms on the market, but nothing I saw really meets all my criteria." Spying a door with a glass panel with the word "pantry" etched into it, he headed toward it. He could use a snack before dinner, 'cause God only knew when that would be served.

"Maybe I can help." Scott Ramsey's voice preceded him down the old servant's staircase and into the kitchen. "I know every piece of land for sale in the area."

"He should," Roseanne said, joining them. "He's been buying it up like they aren't making any more."

"Well, they aren't," Scott said in his defense. "You sure you want acreage? There's more to choose from here in town."

Colin shook his head, his snack forgotten for the moment. "I've thought about it, but no. I need space."

"And some privacy," Becky said. "I've seen the headlines in the trashy magazines. You've become their favorite subject."

He couldn't deny it. The paparazzi were everywhere in Nashville, and if they couldn't uncover a real story, they made one up. "Apparently, I have. Is it too much to ask to just be left alone?"

"Speaking as someone who has had a few run-ins with the kind of people you're talking about," Scott said, "I can sympathize. Since I took myself out of the New York social scene, things have calmed down for me a lot."

Scott was one of *The* Ramsey's—an old money family whose pictures regularly appeared in the social columns. "The key is to fly under their radar. Don't do anything to draw attention to yourself. And, it helps to live in a place like this where they wouldn't normally think to look."

"Unfortunately, Butte Plains is widely known to be my hometown. I never thought to keep it a secret until it was too late. It's only a matter of time before one of those vultures starts wondering where I've gone. That's why I need something with acreage. And a fence."

"There's one place I can think of…if you aren't afraid of a little work."

"I'm pretty good with my hands, and anything I can't do myself, I can afford to hire out now. Where is this place?"

"You know where the Scoggins used to live?" Scott asked.

Colin glanced at Roseanne. "Didn't you say Julie Davis bought the Scoggins place?" Just saying her name made his body react in a most uncomfortable way. Trying to seem casual, he moved to put the kitchen island between them.

"She did," Roseanne said. Concern in her voice, she asked Scott, "She isn't selling, is she?"

"No. No way. She's pretty well ensconced there with the brewery set up and all. I'm talking about the place adjacent to hers. There's an old farmhouse, a couple of barns, and about a hundred acres of pastureland, if I recall correctly. They don't want to break it up into smaller parcels, and there aren't many buyers who want that much land."

"Whose place is it?" Becky asked.

"I can't remember the name," Scott said. "But if Colin is interested, I'll see what I can find out. I don't think it's actually listed for sale."

Living next door to Julie Davis might be the death of him, but with a hundred acres, the likelihood of seeing her, even once in a while, was slim. "I'm interested. See what you can find out."

CHAPTER FIVE

Colin vaguely remembered the Scoggins family farm but knew he'd recognize it if he saw it. Besides, it was a nice day, and what else did he have to do?

With a cup of coffee from the new establishment on Main Street, aptly named Wide Awakenings, he headed out of town, in the opposite direction from the freeway. *The farther off the main roads, the better*, he thought as he passed several new housing developments going up on what had once been farmland. How long would it be before urban sprawl made it out to Julie's place? He didn't know how much land she had, but if he bought the adjacent hundred acres, then she sold out to a developer, he'd be screwed.

As he maneuvered along the winding two-lane farm-to-market road, he recognized several farms he knew had been in the same families for generations. Some had fallen into disrepair, but, for the most part, they hadn't changed a bit since he was a kid growing up in Butte Plains. He wondered how many of the kids who had lived on these farms and gone to school with him had stayed to take on the family business.

Some, perhaps, but it was hard to make a living farming unless you had thousands of acres and deep enough pockets to survive the lean years when crops failed due to drought or too much rain or any of the other million reasons a field might not produce.

Not much different than the music business. Who knew why one song made the charts and stuck, and why another didn't? Hell. Farming might be the way to go, except once a successful crop was sold, that was it. No more income. If you had a record take off, the money kept coming in long after it dropped from the charts.

Just keep on keeping on. Words he'd learned to live by in those early years when he'd first moved to Nashville with nothing more than a handmade guitar and a dream. He was one of the lucky ones who had risen from the masses to make a living doing what he loved. So many of the artists he'd met waiting tables by day and playing dives by night were still there. Caught in a web they couldn't seem to break out of.

He knew the Scoggins place the moment he saw it. The house had been part of the North Texas landscape for over a century, and if he recalled correctly, the youngest of the Scoggins kids had been a year or two ahead of his sister in school. Colin checked his rearview mirror before stopping in the traffic lane to get a good look at the property. A barn, not much newer than the house sat a good distance away. The only new structure, a huge, metal-sided building, sat behind the house.

So, this was the home of Lucky Lady Brewing Company. The only thing setting the place apart from the other old farmsteads he'd passed was the fancy new gate at the end of her paved drive and a small sign bearing the Lucky Lady logo.

Apparently, Julie Davis liked her privacy, too. "A girl after my own heart."

A battered, old farm truck approached from the other direction. Colin checked his rearview again then accelerated, leaving Julie's place behind. A short distance past her driveway was a dirt road with nothing but a couple of strands of barbed wire attached to bois d'arc posts to act as a gate.

Colin pulled off the road and got out. The drive took a sharp turn and disappeared around what appeared to be a natural rise in the land. No structures were visible from the road, at least not from this angle, but he imagined the house and barn were somewhere up there, beyond the rise. Which, if he was right, meant the house couldn't be more than a stone's throw from Julie Davis's house. That gave him pause.

Hoping to get a better look at the house, he returned to his truck and resumed his drive. It wasn't until he'd turned around and headed in the direction he'd come that he spied the house. The old Queen Anne style farmhouse sat exactly where he'd thought. He wouldn't mind having Julie as a neighbor. The gate she'd put up testified to her love of privacy, but what if she expanded the brewery? Besides the paparazzi finding out where he was, the last thing he needed was a large-scale production going on next door. There'd be trucks rolling in, day and night, and workers. *Shit*. It would be a nightmare of the first order.

Or, she could sell to a developer. He'd have tract houses popping up like prairie dogs right next door. He couldn't decide which scenario would be worse.

Maybe this isn't even the place. The house appeared abandoned. The paint was peeling, and if his eyes weren't deceiving him, several windows were broken out. Tufts of grass were coming up in the ruts of the dirt driveway. It was by far the worst looking place he'd seen on this road.

Colin continued on, taking note of the land on the other side of Julie's place. The house on the other property was newer than Julie's, or the one he'd just seen by about a century. Sleek and modern, it was far from abandoned. Miles of fencing divided the place into smaller pastures where horses grazed, each in their own space. Who the heck had that kind of money out here? He'd have to ask Scott. If anyone knew, he would. Despite being a recent transplant to the community, the man seemed to know everything and everyone. In the long run, it didn't really matter who lived there. This wasn't the property Scott had spoken to him about. No way. He'd specifically said there was an old farmhouse, and this one was not old.

Maybe he should look for something else. Living within a stone's throw of Julie's house wasn't the best idea. She obviously didn't want to see him. Sort of awkward since one of the reasons he'd decided to look for a place in Butte Plains was because of her. Colin slapped the steering wheel with the palm of his hand. It was that damned kiss. One fucking kiss, and he'd lost his freaking mind.

In hindsight, perhaps putting her in her car immediately after—without a word, if he recalled correctly—might not have been the right thing to do. But, damn it all to Hell, she'd short-circuited his brain. It's what he told himself, anyway. The truth was too hard to admit in the light of day. Something so profound could only be examined in the darkest part of the night when he was alone with the memories of a perfect sunrise kiss. Then, and only then, did he accept he'd been scared out of his mind.

He'd never felt anything like the feelings that rocketed through him when their lips touched. He'd understood on a cellular level that Julie Davis posed a threat to everything he'd ever wanted. Just one kiss and he knew he'd give up Nashville and his dream of making it big in the country music industry for one night in her bed. He hadn't had much to drink, but his realizations had sobered him up quick, fast, and in a hurry.

Distance hadn't done a thing to dim the memory of the kiss, and time had only given him the opportunity to realize what a complete and utter moron he'd been. On one of those dark and lonely nights, unable to shut the memory down, he'd turned to his guitar. Instead of banishing the memories, they'd come out in the form of words and lines of music he'd written down without even thinking about it. He'd woken up on the sofa the next morning with a sore neck and a hit song to show for it.

Since the release of "Hello, Sunshine, Goodbye," he'd had several tunes hit the top of the charts. His fan base consisted of mostly women, his manager told him, who loved a guy who could admit he'd been wrong. Colin hadn't been wrong, but he'd keep his knowledge to himself. Taking Julie to bed the morning he kissed her *would* have been wrong. She wasn't a one-night-stand kind of woman, and it was all he'd been able to offer her at that time. His career had simply meant too much to him then, and Butte Plains still looked better in his rearview mirror than through the windshield—even if the sexiest woman alive lived there. He'd done what was right for both of them, and, despite the way she'd ditched out on him yesterday at her new tasting room, he still held out hope she'd give him another chance.

❧

"Good news," Scott said as they sat down to another of Roseanne's delicious dinners. It had been nearly a week since he'd promised to inquire about the old farm he'd mentioned to Colin. In the meantime, Colin had looked at several other properties with a local real estate agent and come up empty. Real estate was drying up in Butte Plains, thanks to his sister and her husband. The business they'd resuscitated had infused new life into the entire area. Good for the town, but not so good for him.

"I could use some good news about now."

Scott held the chair for his fiancée then took the one beside her. "I spoke with the owner of the property I told you about the other day. She said she might entertain an offer."

Colin perked up. "Really? Fantastic!"

"She has some conditions, though." He helped himself to a large scoop of mashed potatoes then passed the dish to Colin. "You might not be interested once you hear them."

"I'd agree to just about anything right now. I've looked at half-a-dozen properties this week, and they're all crap." He ticked off their shortcomings. "No land. No house. A contaminated well. Hell, one of them was landlocked. The owner has been fighting to get legal access through a neighboring property for the last thirty years."

"Seriously?" Roseanne passed a basket of homemade rolls. "Can they prevent a person from accessing legally owned property?"

Colin took a couple of warm rolls but kept the basket nearby. "It's some sort of family argument. Began a couple of generations ago, I guess. The land was divided between two brothers who hated each other in hopes they would, as the agent put it, find common ground and learn to get along. They never did. The one with access to his property refused to let his brother clear a road to his property. He even bought all the surrounding property just to spite his brother. The landlocked parcel has since been passed down to another generation, but still no luck in procuring an easement across the relative's land."

"Good luck selling, then," Scott said.

Colin shrugged. "Even if I could get a good look at it, I wouldn't want it. No one has set foot on it since the will was probated. The real estate agent had a satellite photo. It's a mess. Thanks, but no thanks." He bit into one of the fresh rolls and moaned as the buttery yeast flavor burst on his tongue. "I've died and gone to Heaven!"

Roseanne laughed and passed him a dish. "Try it with some of this cinnamon butter."

"Careful, woman. If you keep feeding me like this, I might not ever leave."

"You'll leave," Scott said. "Just wait until the baby gets here. Crying babies and dirty diapers trump food, no matter how good it is."

Colin shuddered and made a face. "Please, spare me! What does the woman want in return for selling the property? I've got cash, and I'm willing to throw in a pint of blood if it will convince her to sell."

"Two conditions. First, you can't bulldoze the house. She wants it restored."

Colin let the first condition sink in. "And?"

"You can't subdivide the land. She doesn't want it turned into a housing development."

"I don't have a problem with keeping all the land, but I need to see the house before I agree to restore it. If it's structurally sound, then I'm willing to talk."

"You should take someone with you to look at the house. Someone who knows what to look for."

Colin raised one eyebrow. "I suppose you know someone?"

Scott smiled. "Yep. Randy Tucker. He's done a lot of work for me, including restoring this house and my new office space downtown. He did the work on the new Lucky Lady Brewing Company tasting room, too."

Having seen two of the three places Scott had listed, Colin didn't need further convincing. "Send me his number."

CHAPTER SIX

Colin wrestled the post and wire gate out of the way. One look at the neglected driveway and he decided to leave his truck where it was and walk up to the house. Fixing the driveway went on his mental list of needed repairs. As he approached the house, he knew the list was going to be a very long one. He didn't need a restoration expert to tell him the porch wasn't safe, and the siding needed paint. One of the two chimneys looked like it might fall at any moment.

While he waited for Randy Tucker to arrive, he moved cautiously from room to room, falling in love a little bit more with each space he entered. He caught a glimpse of something moving outside and went to take a better look. A large black dog dashed across the yard, intent on following the trail of something only he could smell. The dog disappeared into the tall weeds just as another flash of movement caught his eye. Colin smiled as Julie Davis carefully navigated her way through the barbed-wire fence separating the two properties. Dressed in worn denim and a T-shirt bearing the Lucky Lady Brewing

Company logo, her blonde hair pulled into a high ponytail, she took his breath away.

Memories, never far from his thoughts, of the kiss they'd shared came roaring to the forefront with a vengeance. His dick grew hard and his fingers itched to feel the silk of her hair threading through them. He'd have to make peace with her somehow if they were going to be neighbors. He wouldn't apologize for the kiss, but he would apologize for the way he'd sent her off into the sunrise by herself. She deserved to know why he'd done it, even if it meant admitting his cowardice.

Maybe if she knew the truth she'd give him a second chance.

Just as he lost sight of her on the downside of the rise the house sat on, someone rapped on the front door. "Come on in," he called out. "It's open."

Colin nodded at the man who stepped inside. "You must be Randy Tucker. I'm Colin Parker. It's nice to meet you." The two shook hands.

"Same," Tucker said as he took in the once-beautiful home. "This is quite the place. Needs work."

"Tell me something I don't know." Colin laughed. "She looks like she has good bones, but I'm no expert."

"Looks can be deceiving." Tucker ran his hand over a dusty doorframe. "I'll be straight up with you. Even with good bones, this is going to cost a small fortune to restore. It would be cheaper to gut it and start over with new materials than to try to save what's here."

Colin shook his head. "Starting over's not an option. It's either restore it or walk away from the property." He explained about the seller's stipulations.

"Okay, then," Tucker said. "Let's have a look around. I'll take some notes, and I should be able to give you an estimate in a couple of days. Some things will be nonnegotiable, meaning they have to be done for various reasons—to meet current building codes or for safety reasons. Other things will be optional. Maybe you'll want to do them now or wait a while—spread the expense out over a few years."

"You think it'll be that bad?"

"Won't know until I get a better look at the place. Want to show me around?"

They walked through the house. Randy asked questions in each room to determine what Colin hand in mind for each one, offering ideas when Colin came up short on vision. Tucker climbed into the attic then took a look under the house. By the time they were done, their shadows cut a long swath across the front lawn.

"Good news." Tucker stood on the far side of the driveway to get a look at the front elevation. "The structure appears to be sound. I noticed some cracks in the plaster walls, which might mean we need to do some leveling, but we're talking a minor repair compared to having to redo the entire foundation."

"Then I'm not crazy if I buy this place?"

"Not by a longshot. I won't lie. It's going to cost a lot of money to fix it up."

"I've got money. I'd just like to have some left over when I'm done."

Tucker laughed and held out his hand. They shook hands. "I'll call you in a couple of days, and we can get together and review the estimate. Then you can decide if it's the place for you."

"Sounds good." Colin watched as the restoration expert disappeared around the curve in the drive. He didn't want to tell him, but he'd made up his mind to buy the place the minute he saw Julie Davis crawl through the fence.

❧

Julie tallied up the invoices for the third time. Her concentration had been shit this morning, and she knew exactly where to place the blame—on Colin Parker's shoulders. With a little luck, he'd go home to Nashville in a few days. She'd done a credible job of banishing him, and *The Kiss*, from her thoughts over the last few months, but knowing he was in town—and looking for her—had brought those memories back in a rush, making her knees weak and her heart race.

He was bad news. Too good-looking for his own good, he was also a talented singer/songwriter with a huge following. The baseball cap and sunglasses he'd sported at the tasting room hadn't been a fashion statement. They'd been a necessity. They might fool most, but she'd known it was him instantly. He was too popular for his visit not to draw attention soon. Someone would recognize him and word would spread. Before long, the paparazzi would show up, followed by his fans.

"All the more reason for me to stay right where I am until he leaves town, don't you think?" she asked Bud, her black Labrador retriever. The dog, sprawled on the floor at her feet, didn't move a muscle. She reached down and rubbed the top of his head. He opened his eyes and rolled to his side, feet outstretched. "Sorry," she said with a smile. "I hate to disturb your nap, but I could use some fresh air. How about you?"

The dog raised his head then laid down again. Bud wasn't much company, but he was all she had. He listened when she needed someone to talk to, and he never offered his opinion unless treats were involved. Health codes prevented him from being inside the brewing room, but she made up for the time apart by accompanying him on long walks as often as possible. Thanks to her forty acres and the hundred acres adjacent, which had been vacant for at least a decade judging by the decay of the old house on the property, Bud never ran out of things to sniff and places to explore. She'd inquired about buying the adjoining acreage when she'd purchased her place, but the family hadn't been ready to part with the land their ancestors had farmed up until the late 90s. She hated to see the house continue on its downward spiral, but there wasn't anything she could do about it. The owners would sell when they were ready. Not to her, though. She didn't need a second house or more acreage to take care of. The house she had was plenty big enough for one human and one dog, and she had no interest in expanding the brewery beyond its current footprint. With a little luck, her neighbors would sell to someone interested in restoring the house to its former glory. If they let her continue her walks with Bud on the property, she'd consider it a bonus.

"Come on, lazy." Julie stood. "Let's get out of here for a few minutes." The moment her hand touched the door knob, Bud scrambled up and pushed past her, his toenails clicking on the old wood floor. She'd put as much sweat as money into making the small house her own, and she loved every square inch of it. It wasn't huge like the old Victorian next door, but it felt like a mansion compared to the small apartment she'd grown up in. Opening the door to wide-open spaces instead of a busy street lined with ageing apartment buildings and even older businesses never got old.

Julie took a deep breath, filling her lungs with clean air. Satisfied to let Bud lead, she followed him around the house and across to the neighboring property. Once under the sagging barbed-wire fence, he took off running. Julie took her time, carefully maneuvering over the rusted wire. She'd ruined several pieces of clothing, trying to get from one pasture to the next and wasn't ready to ruin another today.

"Bud!" she called. "Wait up!" Unconcerned about the dog—he knew where he was going and how to find his way home—Julie sauntered past the old farmhouse and down the well-worn path the dog had taken. He loved to chase the ducks that called the old stock tank on the property home. They'd never let him catch them, and she doubted he'd know what to do with one if he did catch it. She thought he just liked to see them flap their wings and hear them squawk.

Julie found Bud right where she thought he'd be and sat down on a grassy patch along the bank of the man-made water hole to watch the show. Bud's ears flapped and his tongue lolled out as he danced along the edge of the water, barking at the ducks who had all gathered in the middle of the tank, totally unconcerned for their safety. With any other Labrador retriever, they'd be in trouble, but not with her dog. He had to be the only retriever on the planet who was afraid of water.

"Give it a break, Bud. Maybe they'll come to the bank if you shut up for a little while." As if he understood, the dog stretched out next to her, and, in a few minutes, his snoring brought a smile to her lips. "Good idea," she said, lying on the grass. The paperwork on her desk could wait while she took a few minutes for herself. She closed her eyes and let the peace of the place settle over her.

෫ৠৎ

Colin sat on the steps leading up to the porch and let his imagination take flight. He could see himself sitting here with his guitar, playing for friends or quietly composing in his head. Something about the property lowered his blood pressure, though he knew he'd probably want to blow the house to smithereens long before the renovation was complete. He'd have to find a place to stay until the house was livable. He'd want to keep a close watch on the process, which meant he'd need to be nearby. His gaze swept the open horizon. Other than the old barn, there wasn't a thing in sight. Unless he looked around the corner.

Standing, he stretched then walked around to the side yard to peer at his neighbor's house. It wasn't anywhere as large as this one, but it had to have at least two bedrooms. A smile broke across his face as the craziest idea he'd ever had formed in his mind.

She'd never go for it. Not in a million years, but if there was one thing Colin had learned from his time in Nashville, it was that you didn't get anywhere if you didn't take a risk now and then. Producers and record labels weren't going to find you if you hid in your room, and sexy brewmaster's weren't going to invite you to live in their spare room if you let them run away every time they saw you coming.

He eyed the spot where she'd come through the sagging fence then let his gaze follow the path she'd taken. Unless she'd reentered her property somewhere else, she had to still be on his side of the fence. With his fledgling idea still forming in his head, he set out in the direction he'd last seen Julie Davis' fine ass going. "You can run, but you can't hide, woman."

The trail was nothing more than a path created by feet repeatedly trampling the overgrown grass into submission. Colin mentally added a tractor with a deck mower to his list of necessities. He'd earned extra money in high school, cutting and baling hay for some of the farms in the area. Most of the other teenagers who'd hired on to do the dirty and exhausting work had hated it, but he'd found it oddly soothing. Like everyone else, he'd despised loading the square bales onto a trailer then unloading them again in the barns, but driving the tractor had been fun. The rhythmic swoosh and slice of the mower blades cutting through the dry grass, and the hum of the engine providing a steady backbeat had been music to his ears.

The place would make a great hay farm, he thought as he stood at the edge of the rise the house sat upon and looked out over the rest of the property. It had been cleared for farming except for a spot to the north where a copse of trees remained. Farmers in the early days rarely relied on cash crops to feed their families. They'd purchased staples like flour and sugar but provided their own meat and vegetables. And where there was livestock there was water. He'd bet his new boots those trees surrounded a stock tank.

He knew he'd been right! As he got closer, he felt the dip in temperature and the rise in humidity. His nose twitched at the slightly fishy smell. It wasn't uncommon to have these man-made tanks stocked with channel catfish. The bottom-dwellers supposedly helped keep the water clean by eating everything from dead fish to algae. Catfish were sort of a regional delicacy around these parts, too. Colin had never been a fan of the fish, fried or otherwise, and since he didn't plan to keep livestock, maybe he'd just have the tank filled in. Wondering what the work was going to cost him, and if he could do it himself, he didn't realize how close he'd come to the water until he caught a glimpse of it up ahead. The clear water sparkled like a diamond surrounded by emeralds. The trees he'd seen from the rise would shade the tank in the heat of the day, but, this late in the afternoon, were silent sentinels on the far bank. A wide band of lawn variety green grass carpeted the perimeter of the rocky shoreline. Half-a-dozen white ducks huddled together on the bank opposite while the two interlopers he'd come in search of, apparently unaware of his presence, lay sprawled on the grass not twenty feet from where he stood.

Colin's chest shook with silent laughter. She had some watchdog. He hadn't exactly tried to disguise his approach. Even the ducks had raised their heads to determine the threat posed by his arrival before tucking their bills under their wings to resume their afternoon nap. But not this dog. He hadn't moved an inch. From where he stood, Colin could hear the canine's snores. He shook his head at the sight. What a life. Nothing better to do on a sunny afternoon than trespass on your neighbor's property for a little siesta time.

For about two heartbeats, he considered leaving them to their naps, but he couldn't do it. This time, trying to be as quiet as possible, he moved forward until he could see Julie's face. With no makeup, and relaxed in slumber, she looked like every guy's girl-next-door fantasy come to life. He could attest to the kissability of her lips, and the softness of her curves in his hands. She'd allowed him enough liberties during their one kiss to know her breasts were a perfect handful, and her hips generous enough to hang on to.

God, how he wanted her. Had since he'd first laid eyes on her at his sister's wedding. Kissing her had confirmed everything he'd suspected. She could be *the one*. The realization had been about as frightening then as discovering an alien blob was eating its way through small Texas towns, and Butte Plains was next on the menu.

Adjusting the instant hard-on he'd gotten the minute he saw her, he took a seat beside her. Too far away to touch, but close enough to fuel all manner of fantasies involving him and her and a patch of green grass.

Every soft puff of air from between her lips made him harder. Every tiny movement she made brought on fantasies of her moving beneath him while he made love to her. How could just watching a woman sleep be such torture?

Snapping off a too-long blade of grass, he systematically destroyed it by peeling off one strip at a time until nothing remained but the thick spine down the middle. It was either fidget or kiss his sleeping beauty awake, and he knew one thing for certain. One kiss wasn't going to be enough. Not this time.

He bent to select another blade of grass to torture when she stirred beside him. Snapping off the perfect specimen, a blade about a foot long and nearly an inch wide, he turned. Expecting to find her still asleep, he smiled when, eyes still closed, she stretched her limbs. The thin fabric of her T-shirt pulled tight over her tits, and the hem rose up enough to show a strip of pale skin above the waistband of her jeans.

The blade of grass he'd picked was no match for Colin's fist. *Shit.* Keeping his hands to himself was going to take more self-control than he possessed. But he'd find it somewhere. Like everything else he'd ever decided to do, he wouldn't fail in this. If it took until the end of the world, he'd convince Julie Davis to give him a chance.

CHAPTER SEVEN

Julie stretched as the last remnants of her recurring dream evaporated into what they were—figments of her imagination. Why, oh why did she have to keep reliving *The Kiss*? Her lips remembered it like it had been yesterday, and her subconscious continued to dredge it up on a regular basis—usually when she was tired or stressed. In the dream, they didn't stop with one kiss.

Why couldn't she be one of those people who didn't remember their dreams? She recalled every detail from the feel of his lips on hers, to the heat of his bare skin pressed against hers as they moved together as one. How many times had she woken up with an ache between her legs, reaching for a man who wasn't there? Who never would be. Never *could* be.

The warm earth and soft grass felt good—so good she didn't want to wake up, but she sensed the sun going down, and she didn't want to try to navigate her way home in the pitch black on a trampled grass trail that rambled wherever a certain black lab's nose had taken him.

Recalling the stack of documents she'd left on her desk, she groaned. There was nothing she hated more than sitting at a desk all day, crunching numbers. But with her investment advisor arriving tomorrow, she hadn't had a choice. She needed to know which investments were paying off, and which weren't. Rich people didn't stay rich by sticking their head in the sand. Winning the money had been easy. Keeping it was the trick. Her associate's degree in business wasn't nearly enough to qualify her to manage a billion-dollar estate, but it was all she had to draw upon to wrangle a bevy of lawyers and advisors who profited when she did. So far, they'd all done well. She couldn't complain, but dreams like the one she'd just had could derail her.

Single women everywhere had to be careful. There were all kinds of creeps out there, but as a single woman with money, she had to be even more careful. She'd learned that lesson the hard way. She doubted Colin Parker was out to get her money. Surely, he had plenty of his own since his career had taken off, but damn—*The Kiss*! What she'd give for a do-over. She'd push him away. Tell him to keep his hands and those damn intoxicating lips of his to himself!

She'd been content with her lot in life—resigned to keeping men at arm's length in order to protect her secret. Then Colin Parker had walked into his sister's wedding, and she'd nearly forgotten her self-imposed rules. Recovering just in time, she'd left as early as was socially acceptable, ending up at a new music venue on the outskirts of town. Ironically, the owners were a set of brothers whose criminal records prevented them from selling alcohol. But they'd quickly built a reputation for drawing some of the best musical talent around, and the place was packed most nights. It had been the perfect spot to spend an anonymous evening. Until Colin Parker walked in.

He hadn't been crazy famous then, just up-and-coming famous. The locals who'd recognized him hadn't treated him like the celebrity he was now. In hindsight, it was the he's-no-big-deal attitude that had given her a false sense of security. She'd let him get close. Had danced with him to a couple of songs then ended up talking with him until they'd been kicked out so the brothers could lock up. They'd continued their conversation on the hood of his car. One thing had led to another, which led to *The Kiss*.

A whisper of movement—nothing more than a rumor on the otherwise still air—put all her senses on red alert. She'd seen signs of wildlife in the area. Coyotes weren't unheard of, and the occasional deer. Maybe the water had attracted a raccoon? Could just be one of the ducks looking for bugs in the grass. Lay there and pretend to be asleep, or run for her life?

A shift in the air currents brought an unexpected scent to her nostrils. The only animal who smelled like that was the male of the human species. One particular male to be precise. Heart racing, Julie jerked upright. And there he sat, his gaze heating her from the inside out. Or maybe it was the remnants of her dream talking.

Colin Parker sat a safe distance away—if she were a rabbit, but she couldn't move as fast as the little puffy-tailed fur balls inhabiting the area. If he wanted, he could grab her before she was able to scramble to her feet. Her stupid heart wanted to believe he'd had ample opportunity while she slept to cause her harm, while her brain warned her not to listen to a damn thing her heart had to say. Choosing not to be stupid, she went with her brain.

"Are you stalking me?" she shrieked. She tried to put more distance between them, but Bud, sprawled out on her other side, had no intention of moving. With the water at her feet, she was left with one option. She crab-walked backwards then pushed to her feet.

Colin watched her retreat but made no move to follow her. "Simmer down," he said, turning to face her. "I saw you come this way earlier, and when you didn't return, I thought I'd see if you were still out here."

"Sounds a lot like stalking." Without taking her eyes off him, she moved closer to her dog. Bud raised his head, sniffed the air once then stood. He stretched into a perfect downward dog yoga pose before padding over, tail wagging, tongue hanging out, to nose at Colin Parker.

Petting Bud as if they were the best of friends, Colin glanced up at her. "Stalking implies I've been following you, and I have not. I was minding my own business when you trespassed on my property. I simply wanted to make sure you had returned home safely."

"Wha-what do you mean, *your* property?"

Colin pushed Bud off his lap and stood. Brushing dog hair and grass from his jeans, he said, "Well, it's not mine yet, but it will be soon. I've decided to buy this place."

Her mind raced to make sense of what he'd just said. "I didn't know it was for sale." Was that the best she could come up with?

Colin shrugged. "Officially it's not, but the owner is willing to sell to the right person."

"And you're the right person." Julie snickered. "Yeah, right."

"Apparently, I am. I've agreed to her price contingent on being able to meet her conditions. I came out today to see if the house could be restored. I saw you from the kitchen window when you came through the fence."

"That was hours ago."

"I told you, I was checking out the house. Even had a restoration expert out to take a look." He tucked his hands in the front pockets of his jeans and looked a little embarrassed. "It needs *a lot* of work."

She hadn't been inside, but she saw the outside every day. The exterior was enough to scare most buyers off. She called Bud to her side and began walking up the path the two of them had made through the tall grass. She didn't look to see, but knew Colin followed. When the old house came into view, she stopped. "Is it worth saving?"

Colin stopped beside her. "Randy Tucker says it is."

"Did he also tell you it's going to cost a fortune?"

"He did. I won't know an amount for a few days, but I suspect his estimate is going to make my checkbook weep."

Julie laughed, listening to her heart this time. He hadn't been stalking her. Her brain argued with her again. "Why this house, this place? There must be others that don't need this much work."

"I should have bought something last year, but coming home was the last thing on my mind at the time. Since then, the real estate market has dried up. People are snatching up everything in sight. Scott Ramsey told me about this place, said he knew the owner. So, here I am, looking to buy an extreme fixer-upper."

"You said the seller has conditions?"

"She wants it in the contract that the buyer has to restore the house. She doesn't want it torn down or left to fall down. And, she doesn't want the land sold off or subdivided."

"As your future neighbor, I hope you agree to her conditions."

"I will. Randy assured me the house is sound despite all appearances to the contrary."

"He does good work."

"I'm staying with Scott and Roseanne. He did a beautiful job on their old house, and I saw what he did with your tasting room."

"You've been there?" she asked.

"You know I was."

"If you're implying *I'm* stalking *you*—"

"I saw you hightailing it out of there a few minutes after your bar girl went looking for you."

Heat crept into her cheeks. She didn't know what to say, so she kept her mouth shut.

"I don't blame you. I wouldn't want to see me either if I were you."

He was right, she'd been avoiding him, but she'd like to know why he thought she was. "Why would you think I'm avoiding you?"

For the first time since they'd been standing there, he turned his attention away from the house to look at her. "I'm sorry, Julie. If I had it to do over again, I would have put you in my car and taken you back to the B&B with me. Sending you home alone after…well, after that kiss was the cowardly thing to do."

Her brain decided enough was enough. Her stupid heart was going to get her in big trouble with this man if she didn't watch out. For crying out loud, he was going to be her neighbor! She had to keep their relationship in perspective. Telling him she'd been hurt and disappointed, and that her subconscious had repeatedly gone where she physically hadn't, wouldn't do. Instead, she mustered every bit of fake indignation she could come up with and prayed he wouldn't see through her pathetic attempt at acting. Chin held high, she said, "It was the right thing to do. I hate to deflate your giant ego, but I wouldn't have gone with you."

Liar. Liar. Liar. Her heart kept up the mantra all the way to the fence and across her yard to her back door. She certainly would have gone with the up-and-coming country musician, but there was no way she was going to make the mistake of falling for the man he was now. He came with a cruise ship full of baggage, all labeled *paparazzi*, and Lord knew, she had enough baggage of her own. She didn't need any of his.

❧

"Well, that went well," Colin said to his new old house as Julie Davis disappeared inside her own. He hadn't jumped her, and she hadn't run. Small victories, but he'd take them. She was lying when she said she wouldn't have gone to the B&B with him. He'd bet his first platinum record she would have. She'd been as into their kiss as he had been, and he knew willing when he saw it. She'd been willing. If not for the yellow streak down his back, he would have taken her to bed somewhere. Maybe not at the B&B since he'd left the place without a door key, but somewhere.

Colin had to turn on his headlights in order to see how to fasten the rickety gate in place. He mentally added proper lighting to the electric gate and new fencing he'd need. He'd probably dream of dollar signs stalking him tonight. Fiduciary

61

nightmares would be better than dreaming about kissing Julie again. If he'd never kissed her in the first place he'd still be in Nashville, living the carefree life of a bachelor—albeit a poor one.

He let himself in to Scott and Roseanne's house with the key Roseanne had given him and made his way up to his room on the third floor. He'd chosen one at the rear of the house partly because it was decorated in shades of green, and partly because his hosts' bedroom was one floor below on the front of the house. He'd thought this would be better than staying in his sister's small house with her and her new husband, but Scott and Roseanne weren't much better. They weren't newlyweds, but they were more lovey-dovey than he'd expected them to be, given Roseanne's pregnancy.

Tossing his keys on the dresser, he sat on the edge of the bed and pulled off his shoes. He'd made progress today on two fronts. He'd found a place to live. Granted, it was a dump, but Randy had convinced him it could be saved. And, he'd apologized to Julie.

They were on speaking terms now—a plus in his book. Convincing her to let him bunk at her place while his was under construction was going to take some doing. She had every right to be wary of his intentions because his intentions were questionable.

He intended to have her in his bed. From there, the intentions were quite clear in his head. He'd honed them in his dreams every night since the kiss. He knew exactly how he'd strip her clothes off her. He knew exactly how he would tease her nipples and drive her to the edge with his fingers between her legs. He knew every way he would make love to her.

God, he was hard just thinking about touching her. And, he was damned tired of fucking his hand instead. His newfound fame brought a lot of unwanted attention from his female fans. He couldn't count the number he'd declined to sleep with over the last few months. They were everywhere, seemingly crawling out of the woodwork in restaurants and outside the local venues he loved to play. Some had even found out where he lived and shown up on his doorstep. He'd turned them all down because of a memory he couldn't banish no matter how hard he tried.

He should have known Julie Davis wasn't like the others. His success didn't impress her because she'd taken the time to actually get to know him. Her opinion of him wasn't based solely on the lyrics of a song he'd written. Unfortunately, the opinion she had of him wasn't a good one. Why else would she have gone out of her way to avoid him?

As he headed to the shower in the en suite bathroom, he hoped his apology today had elevated her opinion of him.

CHAPTER EIGHT

"Colin!" Becky rolled away from her desk and stood. "What brings you by?"

It was the first time he'd been to her office since he'd returned. Adams Manufacturing seemed to grow larger by the day. He took in his surroundings. She'd redecorated since his last visit the week of her wedding. "Not much." He chose one of the fancy upholstered chairs facing her and sat. "Thought I'd stop by and say hello."

His sister cocked her head to one side. "What's going on, baby brother?"

"What makes you think anything is going on?"

"Get real, Colin. You hate places like this." She waved her hand around to indicate her office. "You're allergic to corporate America. Last time you were here you said the walls gave you hives."

"You said you'd redecorated. I had to come see, didn't I?" He loved messing with her. Always had. She was so easy to rile. The last time he'd been here she'd been anxious about what her wedding guests were going to say once they found out the event they were attending wasn't the real thing. He didn't think anyone would care one way or the other, so to distract her, he'd made the crack about her ugly, outdated office. The strategy had worked. She'd gone into big-sister lecture mode, and, as he'd predicted, the wedding guests thought the video of their secret Vegas nuptials they played at the reception was a hoot. Elvis impersonators tended to make people smile.

"Not buying it. Come on, spill."

He grinned. "Or what? You'll get out the thumb screws?"

"We have something similar," she said. "I'm sure with a little adjustment—"

"Don't say it!" he begged. Just thinking about some of the possible words that could come out of his sister's mouth made him cringe. He'd come to terms with her selling sex toys, but he sure as heck didn't want to talk about them with her. "Please don't say whatever it is you were going to say."

"Then tell me."

"Okay, okay." She'd won the first round. "I bought a house this morning."

Her squeal had him covering his ears. As she rounded the desk, arms spread wide, he stood and allowed her to grab him in a bear hug. He hugged her just as hard, happy she shared his excitement.

"Whoa, there. Who said you could hug my wife?"

At the sound of Ford's voice, Colin placed a kiss on his sister's head then set her away before turning to his brother-in-law who leaned against the doorjamb, a huge smile on his face. "She hugged me first." Colin moved to shake hands with the older man. "Good to see you again."

"Likewise." His gaze slipped to his wife. "What was that high-pitched shriek about?"

Becky wrapped an arm around Ford's waist and kissed him on the cheek. "Baby brother bought a house today! He's back in Butte Plains for good!" She turned her no-nonsense gaze on Colin. "You are staying for good, aren't you? This isn't just an investment?"

Colin nodded. "Yep. I'm here for good. It's going to be a while before I can move in, though. The house needs extensive renovations."

Becky wanted all the details, so, over coffee in the employee break room, Colin filled them in on the property and his agreement to renovate the dilapidated house.

"Sounds like you'll have your hands full for a while." Ford stood and stretched. "Glad to have you home." He glanced at his watch. "I've got a meeting in a few minutes. You'll let me know if you need anything?"

"Sure thing." They shook hands, and Ford left.

"You can count on me, too," Becky said. Colin stood when she did. "I need to get back to work, too." She hugged him again. "I'm so glad you came by to tell me. Mom's going to be so excited. She's missed you."

"She was the first one I told, and yeah, she's glad I'm home, too."

They stopped outside the door to Becky's office. "Seriously, Colin. If you need anything—"

"I'll let you know. I promise."

જ૯૭

The place was officially his. Colin sat on the porch of his new home, looking out at the overgrown landscape because it was the least daunting of possible views. This, he could do something about. He'd nearly bought out the local hardware store this morning, filling up the bed of the new pickup truck he'd purchased just before leaving Nashville. While the grading crew worked on getting the driveway ready for construction vehicles and delivery trucks to access the property, he planned on taming the yard. His new tractor and deck mower would be delivered in a few days. Then he'd tackle the rest of the property. Once the yard was cleared and he could see what he had, he'd decide if he needed to install some privacy landscaping along with the new horse fencing and electronic gate he'd already contracted.

First things first. He unloaded a giant rubber trash can from his truck and began filling it with the debris he could see—plastic bags that had blown in from the road—faded soda cans and beer bottles, evidence the abandoned house had been scouted out by the local teenagers at one time.

After gathering up all the trash he could see, he unloaded the self-propelled mower he'd bought and went to work on the yard surrounding the house. It was slow going, but the blades did a good job of knocking down the knee-high vegetation, which he had to admit was more weeds than grass. Something else to add to the landscaping list, he thought.

❧

Julie glanced at the clock on the nightstand and groaned. Nine a.m. She rolled over and stuffed a pillow over her head to muffle the noise coming from next door. Normally, she'd have been up for hours, checking on the brewing vats, but last night had been another one of *those* nights. Colin Parker and his infernal kiss had invaded her dreams, and she'd woken in the middle of the night, hot, horny, and unable to get back to sleep until nearly dawn.

The sound of a lawn mower, punctuated by the occasional clunk followed by a loud curse, finally drew her out of bed and to the window. Her room, located at the rear of the house above the kitchen, overlooked the neighboring property.

A shiny new red pickup truck sat in front of the old barn. "I guess he really did buy the place," she said to Bud who sat in the middle of her bed watching her and probably wondering when she was going to take him out to do his morning duty. She was about to oblige him when Colin Parker, walking behind a lawn mower, turned the corner of his new house.

"Oh. My. Lord." Jesus, did he have to mow shirtless? Quickly, she stepped to the side so he wouldn't see her ogling his wide shoulders and six-pack abs. He looked even better than her subconscious had imagined he would look, and she'd thought she'd done a pretty good job, based on her limited exposure to the man. "Honey," she said to herself, "you weren't even close."

He got to the corner of the house then turned the mower, cut a swath over to the driveway before turning toward the front of the house again. Julie knew she should look away, but the view from the back was as mesmerizing as the view from the front. Wide shoulders tapered to a slim waist, and, Lord have mercy, a fine ass encased in tight denim! She sighed. Why couldn't the place have sold to a hairy, pot-bellied, tobacco-chewing farmer instead? Those images might have given her nightmares, but she'd take them over the dreams she knew she'd be having based on her new knowledge of his anatomy.

Bud stood and wagged his tail. "Okay. Okay. Give me a minute to put on something decent," she said. "Then I'll take you out. But no going next door. Do you hear me?"

She was watching her first cup of coffee dribble into her favorite mug when she heard another clunk, followed by an even louder clunk which was followed by a curse loud enough to be heard by people in town. Just as she grabbed her mug, the mower cut off. Silence. Blessed silence. Opening the door, she stood aside as Bud rushed out. He wasted no time hoisting his hind leg to do his business against the Rose of Sharon bush. Then he was off like a rocket, headed for the fence separating her place from Colin's.

"Bud!" She raced down the steps and across the yard. "Come back here this minute!"

By the time she reached the fence line, her dog stood next to her new shirtless neighbor. His hand was on Bud's head, giving the dog the attention he sought, but the man's gaze was on the door of his new pickup.

Julie managed to avoid the sharp barbs and got through the fence without tearing her clothes. "I'm sorry," she said as she approached the two. "Bud doesn't have any manners."

Colin continued to look at the truck as he replied, "He's a good dog. Not a problem."

"Well, he shouldn't just run up and demand to be—" Her gaze followed Colin's. "Oh! That's not good."

"Hit a damned rock," he said.

"I heard." Fine lines radiated out from the point of impact to create a sunburst effect on the grapefruit-sized dent in the door panel. "It can be fixed, can't it?"

"Yeah, it can. Just thought it would be a while longer before I dented it up."

"Welcome to life on a farm," she said. "Have you seen my truck? I left it out in a hailstorm last summer. It looks like a giant golf ball now."

The corners of his lips lifted slightly, and, for the first time since she'd joined him, he tore his gaze away from the damage to his vehicle and onto her instead. His blue eyes seared her skin as they traveled from her toes to her nose, while his smile grew broader. His laugh was deep and genuine. "That's yours?"

Julie nodded.

"Damn near laughed my head off when I saw it in town the other day. You should park it inside."

She pointed at the dent in his brand-spanking-new truck. "And you should take your own advice, neighbor."

Colin looked at her as if deciding if she was serious or not. Then his smile grew even wider. "Touché, neighbor. Maybe we could get a package deal on detached garages." He pointed at the old barn. "I need the barn for my tractor and stuff."

"And I have a garage. I'd left the truck out because I knew I'd need it later on. The storm took me by surprise. Luckily, my Camaro was in the garage."

"There go my plans to try to get a two-for-one deal on a garage." He didn't look the least bit disappointed.

"Maybe you can negotiate a deal for a new barn *and* a new garage?"

"Or maybe I'll have a garage added onto the recording studio I'm going to have built."

"Recording studio?" Images whirled through her mind like a tornado on steroids. People coming and going at all hours. Loud music, and God knew what all.

"Yeah. I need a place to work. You didn't think I was retiring, did you?"

She didn't know what she thought, but she knew she hadn't considered the possibility he'd be recording next door to her. "No. I guess… Well, I guess I thought you'd record in Nashville, or at least in Dallas. Not here." She let her gaze wander past the old barn to the expanse of open land. "Where are you planning to put this studio?"

He must have picked up on the tone of her voice because his reply sounded a bit defensive and his smile had vanished. "Why? Afraid you'll have to listen to some country music?"

Country music star or not, she had a right to know what his intentions were since they were neighbors. "I like country music, but I don't want to listen to it all night. Some of us have to sleep, you know."

"Duly noted. I'll make sure the banjo-playing rednecks are off the front porch at a decent hour."

Infuriating man. Julie planted her fists on her hips and glared at Colin. "You know that's not what I meant, but thanks anyway." She glanced at the dent one more time. "And try to keep the cursing down, too, while you're at it."

The damned fence snagged her blouse as she went through. She swallowed a curse rather than give him the satisfaction of knowing how little his cursing had actually bothered her. She'd found it amusing, but she'd never tell him. The arrogant bastard. Why, oh why had she ever thought he could be *the one?*

Not in a million years. Not if he was the last man on the planet. Not if...well, not if!

CHAPTER NINE

That hadn't gone well.

Colin jerked his gaze from the spot in the fence where Julie Davis, her dog, and her fine ass had just gone through. Raking a hand through his hair, he dislodged several pieces of grass then kicked the dent in his door for good measure. "Well, fuck!"

Damn it all to hell. What had begun as a day full of promise had deteriorated at record speed.

Lowering the tailgate, he pulled a water bottle from the cooler he'd brought along and sat down. It wasn't even 10 a.m. and he was sweating like a pig. He'd caused serious damage to his new truck and pissed off the one person in Butte Plains he seriously did not want to piss off. Not only was she his neighbor, which called for diplomacy, but he'd damn near hung the "the one" label on her. He glanced at his watch. Yep. The driveway people were late. He couldn't wait to see what else this day had in store for him.

The cold water felt good as it went down. He finished off the bottle and got another one which he pressed to the back of his neck. It had been a long time since he'd worked this hard, and then he'd done it for the money. No one was paying him to do this, so why was he killing himself? His gaze swept the yard. Weeds and all, it looked a hundred times better without the trash and the overgrown grass. If he tried real hard, he could envision the house the way it had looked in the drawing Randy Tucker had done to illustrate the changes he wanted to make.

New porch posts and railings. New steps. New, energy-efficient windows, custom-made to look identical to the existing ones. A new paint job. And those improvements were just the beginning. Gutters. Roofing. New siding where he'd found dry rot and termite damage. He'd even sketched out a new landscaping plan and recommended a local guy to do the work.

Thus, Colin was out here putting in sweat equity. The landscaper's quote just to clean up the yard—never mind create new flowerbeds and repair the crumbling walkways—had been a shock. Thus the pickup load of lawn and garden equipment and the sweat. Whatever he saved on the yard he could put into the house.

He finished off the second water bottle then tossed the empties into the almost-full trash can.

The driveway contractor arrived just as he finished mowing. After talking to the supervisor to make sure they were on the same page about what was to be done, Colin assembled his new weed whacker. If his neighbor was afraid his music would be too noisy, she probably wasn't too happy right now, either. Between the whir of the weeder's gas engine and the heavy equipment blading the drive, even he was wishing for a set of noise-cancelling headphones.

∾

Colin walked into the Lucky Lady Brewing Company Tasting Room, his gaze sweeping the tables for Scott Ramsey and Ford Adams. His brother-in-law had called earlier and invited him to join them for a beer. Craving some normalcy in his life, he'd grabbed his Mustangs baseball cap and a pair of sunglasses, and headed out.

Spotting them sitting at the table farthest from the wide windows, he smiled and joined them. "Hey." Taking off his sunglasses but leaving the hat on, he sat with his back to the room. He'd let his hair grow some since he'd been home and it now curled up at his collar. His ratty T-shirt bearing the Butte Plains Farmers logo labeled him a local as opposed to a celebrity. As a disguise, it would have to do.

"Hey, yourself." Scott lifted the mug in front of him. "We got a head start. Hope you don't mind."

"Not at all."

Avery, the bartender who he'd met the time he'd come in looking for Julie, appeared at his elbow. "What can I get you?"

Colin glanced at the menu inside a plastic stand situated in the center of the table. "I'll try the Kissed by Sunrise again."

"Coming right up."

"Again?" Ford asked.

Colin shrugged. "I came in here right after I got home. Thought I'd give the place a try."

"It's become a favorite for locals and tourists," Scott said. "Just as I predicted."

"You had something to do with this?" Colin waved his had to indicate the tasting room. It was quickly filling up with the after-work crowd.

Scott explained how he'd pitched the idea to Julie. "She didn't want to do it, but I convinced her she could run it from behind the scenes. Looks like it's paying off for her."

"I would say so," Ford said. "You have to get here early if you want a table."

"How's the house coming?" Scott asked, changing the subject.

Ever since construction had begun on his house, Colin answered more questions than a two-year-old could ask. "Good, I guess. I don't have anything to compare with, though." He frowned as his phone vibrated in his pocket. Reaching for it, he asked, "Is it normal to have to answer a zillion questions a day?"

"Pretty much," Scott said. "You going to answer that?" He pointed to the phone Colin held in his hand.

"I think I'll finish my beer first. Every time they call, I have to drop what I'm doing and drive out there to take a look. Wish I could just delegate the responsibility, but I'm sure I'd live to regret it if I did."

"Why aren't you staying in the house?" Ford took a long drink from his glass.

"You haven't seen the place," Colin said. "It's a dump. They've stripped out all the electrical and plumbing. Dust everywhere. I have to wear a mask just to walk through the rooms." God only knew what was in the dust. He didn't want to sound like a prima donna, but he couldn't risk his voice by breathing in toxic waste.

"What about renting a travel trailer?" Scott waved at a couple who'd just walked in. Colin had never seen them before. Did the man know everyone in Texas? "You'd have all the comforts of home but still be on-site," he continued.

"When I'm on tour, I practically live in one of those things. Don't know if I could stand it as long as the renovation might take. I thought about trying to rent a room from my new neighbor, but I don't think she's too happy with me right now."

Both men stared at him.

"What?"

"What did you do to piss Julie off?" Scott asked.

"Wait." Ford held up one hand. "Julie Davis is your neighbor?"

"Yeah. Her property adjoins mine on the south side. I could throw a rock from my backyard and hit her house." He turned to Scott. "Let's just say, she's not happy having me as a neighbor."

"Huh." Scott took a sip of his beer.

"You could always put up a tent. Camp out," Ford said. "Maybe she'll feel sorry for you and let you rent a room."

Colin froze, his beer halfway to his lips. "You're a genius! Why didn't I think of that?"

"Are you nuts?" Scott's raised voice drew stares from the other customers. "You've got hot and cold running water, a soft bed, and air-conditioning at our place."

"I know, it's crazy, but it might work."

Scott stared at him. "This is about more than being close to the work site, isn't it?"

"Maybe," Colin conceded. He spoke to Ford. "You think the new sporting goods place down the street sells tents?"

"Probably, but if you're looking for sympathy, you don't want to look too comfortable."

"True."

"I've got just the tent you need," he said. "Finish your beer and I'll show you."

"How old is this thing?" Scott held a handkerchief over his nose as they stared at a rotting bundle of canvas in the cobweb-infested basement of Ford's ancestral home.

"Twenty-five years, I guess. My dad bought it when I was a kid. We were going to do the whole family camping thing, but my mom refused to go. I set it up a few times in the yard, but, other than my solo adventures, it hasn't been out of the basement."

"It's perfect." Colin dragged it to the edge of the shelf. "Help me get it out of here."

"I'll hold the door for you," Scott said.

CHAPTER TEN

It had been nearly a week since her dust-up with Colin, and the construction noise was driving her straight up the wall. The sun was barely up when Julie opened the door to let Bud out and found a plastic grocery bag hanging from the handle of her storm door. Still in her summer pajamas, which consisted of a worn-out tank top and a pair of boxer-style shorts, she made sure none of the guys working on Colin's house were looking then stepped out on the porch to grab the bag.

While the dog took care of his business, she went inside and opened the bag. She couldn't help but smile at what she found inside—a pair of noise-cancelling headphones!

She had to give the man credit, he knew how to apologize. She'd often wished she had a pair when she was trying to study while her mother watched television in the other room. The fancy headphones had been way out of her budget then, so she'd made do with a cheap pair of earbuds from the discount store. She hadn't thought about them in ages—well, not since she'd moved here. Up until Colin bought the place next door, she'd had no need for them. With all the construction going on within spittin' distance of her house, she could put them to good use.

Bud scratched at the door, wanting in and to have his breakfast. Still smiling over the headphones, she opened the door. The dog flew in, tail wagging in anticipation of being fed. "Wait just a sec," she said to her loyal canine, her full attention trained on her neighbor's yard. "What the heck does he think he's doing?"

Just then Colin looked up from his task and waved.

Julie waved back then, realizing she was still in her pj's, she jumped inside and slammed the door.

After measuring kibble into Bud's bowl, she ran upstairs to dress. Ten minutes later, she was standing on her side of the fence, watching the famous country music star erect a canvas monstrosity in his yard. "What's the tent for?" she asked when he finished pounding a stake in the ground.

"It's my temporary residence," he said as if living in a tent made perfect sense. "Until the house is livable. Randy says it'll be a couple of months, maybe three."

"You're going to live in a tent for two or three months? That's crazy."

"I don't have many options. I need to be close to the construction. They're really trying to get it just the way I want it, so there are lots of questions to answer. Most of the time, I can't visualize the problem over the phone, so I end up driving out here to take a look. I'm wasting their time and mine, so I decided to camp here. This way, I can work on the landscaping when I want to and do my own thing the rest of the time."

"What are you, nine years old?" She eyed the structure. It could sleep at least ten people and was tall enough in the center even Colin could probably stand up inside it. "Reliving your childhood?" Yeah, it looked older than both of them combined.

"Hey, my family had a lot of fun in this tent when Becky and I were kids. It brings back fond memories. So, yes, maybe I'll be reliving my childhood for a few months, but that's not necessarily a bad thing in my book."

"Seriously, Colin?" The thing couldn't possibly still be waterproof, and there was a tear in one of the screens. She pointed it out. "The mosquitos and God knows what else are going to eat you alive. Not to mention you have no place to shower. What will you do for food?"

"No worries." He dug around in a plastic storage container sitting off to one side for a minute then stood, brandishing a roll of thick tape. "I've got duct tape! Do you have any idea how useful this stuff is?"

Oh, she knew. Nearly everything she'd owned had been held together by duct tape at one time or another. Replacing items had been a last resort, and, even then, they'd often had to decide if they could live without the item or not before sacrificing the funds to buy a new one. More often than not, the new one had come from a thrift store. "You've lost your mind," she said, turning and stomping home. She was going to laugh her head off the first night he ended up sleeping in his pickup because his ancient tent leaked like a sieve.

જાજ

Colin watched his new neighbor stomp off in a huff. He'd got her good. This wasn't the same tent his family had used for their camping trips when he was a kid, but it was about the same age and twice as big. Some of his other camping supplies he'd found in his mother's garage, like the old camp stove and gas lantern, while the cot, sleeping bag, and new battery-operated lantern were purchases he'd made at the new outdoor supply store about a block down from Lucky Lady Brewing Company's tasting room on Main Street.

He'd told Julie the truth about the questions. They *were* driving him nuts, and because he often couldn't imagine what they were trying to get across to him over the phone, he spent way too much time on the road between here and Roseanne and Scott's house.

He'd rolled into town with a week's worth of clothes and the same guitar he'd left with all those years ago. Only the vehicle was different. Not sure the old pickup he'd restored in high school would make the return trip, he'd purchased a new one and made the drive rather than risk someone recognizing him at an airport or rental car company. The rest of his stuff, including the old pickup, would be here when they got here.

In the meantime, he'd be perfectly happy camping out. He had everything he needed, including peace and quiet every night after the workers left. He could roam the property for inspiration or get out his guitar to amuse himself. Hell, he might even find a new song or two if he looked inside himself hard enough. But most of all, he'd be close to Julie.

Once the tent was up and furnished to meet his needs, he went to work on the landscaping in the backyard. After removing the old clothesline, he cut down the shrubs that had grown high enough to block the light to some of the downstairs' rooms.

Colin used the hem of his T-shirt to wipe sweat from his eyes then grabbed a cold water bottle from his cooler.

"Wow. The yard sure looks better." Randy Tucker, restoration expert extraordinaire, stood at the corner of the house looking like the professional delegator he was. "I saw the light coming in through the windows and had to come take a look."

"Thanks." Colin twisted the cap off the bottle and downed half the contents. "Think they'll grow back or should I yank the trunks out and start over?"

"If this was my place, I'd remove the trunks then you can train the new plants to the shape and size you want them."

"I was afraid you were going to say that." He finished off the water then chucked the empty bottle into a nearby trash can. He counted the stumps crowding the foundation. "It's going to take forever to dig all those out."

"You could hire it done," Randy said.

"I could. Or I could enlist some help."

Randy took a step back. "Don't look at me. I've got workers to supervise."

Colin laughed. "Nah. Wasn't thinking of you."

"Whew." Randy wiped imaginary sweat from his brow. "What's with the tent?"

"It's my new home until you get my house finished, so make it quick, will ya?"

"Why didn't you rent a motor home or a travel trailer?"

"I figured it would feel too much like being on tour, and that's one of the things I'm trying to get away from." And, no one, especially not Julie Davis, was going to feel sorry for a guy living in an expensive motor home with all the amenities. But Tucker didn't need to know all Colin's reasoning.

"Okay. Have it your way, but your tent looks like it could leak."

Colin eyed the old canvas structure. It probably did leak. In fact, he was counting on it. "You think?"

"Wouldn't surprise me in the least." The contractor shook his head. "Well, I've got to get to work. Gotta take some measurements so I can get my carpenter started on those new kitchen cabinets."

"Don't let me keep you, then." He waved his hand toward the tent. "As you can see, there's not a minute to waste."

"You might want to reconsider the motor home idea," he called over his shoulder.

Colin shook his head, a smile on his lips. Nah. The tent was perfect. Besides, he was counting on Julie being neighborly and not letting him suffer out here for long.

CHAPTER ELEVEN

Colin leaned on the handle of his shovel and wiped sweat from his brow. When he'd come up with the idea to camp out in his yard, he'd expected the adventure would last a few days before a Texas-sized rainstorm would convince Julie to let him stay in her spare bedroom until his house was habitable. He should have consulted a meteorologist. Then he would have known the weather gods had other plans. Texas was known for its rapidly changing weather. So, where the hell was it?

He downed his third bottle of water that morning and scanned the bright-blue skies. Not a cloud in sight. He'd strip naked and dance around the yard chanting if he thought it would break this cycle of relentless heat.

"How's it going?"

Colin turned to greet the man in charge of restoring the house. "You tell me."

"The house is coming along. We should be finished on schedule." Randy Tucker's gaze swept over the yard. "The patio looks good. The fire pit was a good idea."

"Thanks." He'd spent the better part of the last week on his knees, laying the individual paving stones for the fire pit and patio. "I've got friends coming over tomorrow night for a little informal get-together. There'll be beer, hot dogs, and maybe a song or two. Stop by around seven. Oh, and it's BYOLC."

Tucker frowned. "What's BYOLC?"

Colin smiled. "Bring your own lawn chair. The new patio furniture won't be here until next week." He lifted his shovel and jammed the tip into the hard-packed earth. "With a little luck, I'll have the pergola up by then."

"You're still determined to do this yourself?"

The physical activity was the only thing keeping him from thinking about his sexy neighbor all day long. He hadn't seen much of her since the day he'd put the tent up. Her dog still came over now and then, always stopping for a pet before heading to the pond to chase the ducks. "Once I get the holes dug for the posts, I have some old friends who are going to help me build the structure."

"Do any of you know what you're doing?"

Colin shrugged. "Maybe. Maybe not. Bobby and Tommy will be here tomorrow night. I'm sure they'd appreciate any tips you might be able to give them."

"Bobby and Tommy Watson? The guys who own the music store in town?"

"Yeah. You know them?"

"We haven't officially met, but I've been to their after-hours event a few times."

The Watson twins had gotten into a spot of trouble after high school and spent a while in jail. When they got out, they opened a music store in the old gas station their grandpa left them. They made a decent living these days selling instruments and giving lessons. On weekends, weather permitting, they hosted local talent on a stage they'd built behind the store. The kiss that changed his life took place in the Music City parking lot. The brothers' criminal records kept them from getting a liquor license, but the lack of alcohol hadn't hurt their business. "We all graduated high school together. Used to get together and play music. When my mom would kick us out of our garage, we'd go to theirs, and vice-versa. I can guarantee you, if they get to pickin' tonight, the music will be good."

"I'll think about it." Randy gestured at the house. "I'd better get back to work. Guy who owns this place is chompin' at the bit to move in."

With a smile, Colin bent to his task. He had a pickup load of shrubs to put in before his friends arrived for tonight's cookout.

๛

Julie crooked her finger, pulling the edge of the curtain just enough to sneak a peek at her sexier-than-hell neighbor. Again.

Damn. This was getting to be a habit. She'd lost count of the number of times she'd dropped everything to spy on Colin this week. At first, she told herself she was checking to see how the landscaping was coming along, but peeking once a day would have been more than enough to satisfy her curiosity as to what plants he was putting where.

Nope. This was more than idle curiosity. This was lust. Pure and simple. Well, maybe not *pure*. That would be stretching things a bit too far. She'd had more impure thoughts this past week than in all her adult life combined. Why did the man have to be so good-looking? And fit. He wasn't a rhinestone cowboy. Not with muscles like the ones she'd been admiring all week. A physique like his came from good old-fashioned hard work.

She had to admit, he'd done an excellent job with the landscaping, which appeared to be almost finished. Good thing, too. She'd lost too much time peeking out her bedroom window. When he put the last of the new shrubs in, he'd move on to the front of the house. Out of sight. And hopefully, out of mind.

Like she could forget him. She'd be doing ordinary things—like picking up a case of empty beer bottles—when an image of Colin bent over, laying brick pavers in an intricate pattern around the fire pit would pop into her mind. Then she'd spend the next hour reviewing every mental image she had of the man. He'd even invaded her sleep, starring in the most erotic dreams she'd ever had.

Julie watched him dig the last hole and pop the plant in. All the while, she told herself the show was coming to a close. Might as well watch until the end. Right?

"Probably smells to high heaven," she grumbled to Bud who had followed her upstairs and now was sound asleep on the rug next to her bed. "Just look how dirty and sweaty he is." She shook her head as he wiped his brow on a sleeve then went down on his knees and began to backfill the hole by hand. "He'll never get the dirt out from under his fingernails."

But, damn, he had a fine ass. Even if it was encased in filthy denim.

Disgusted with herself, she let the curtain fall from her fingertips. She'd just tidy up a bit before going downstairs.

As she gathered the dirty towels and clothes she'd left scattered about and piled them into a basket to take downstairs, she congratulated herself on her willpower. And look, hadn't she turned an unscheduled looky-loo trip upstairs into something useful? She grabbed a soft cloth from the linen cabinet and began to dust her bedroom furniture. When she got to her nightstand, her arm brushed the window curtain aside— just enough. And just in time.

Colin held the water hose in one hand and, with the other, whipped his dirty T-shirt off and turned the water on himself. Julie gave up all pretense and stared. Water cascaded over his head, over his wide shoulders, and down. Down. Down his sexy-as-hell back. Washing away the dirt and sweat. Leaving a wide expanse of firm, tanned, wet skin over flexing muscles as he rinsed his hair.

It wasn't the well water, which she knew would be cold, making her shiver, but the raw masculinity on display. She crushed the edge of the curtain with fingers itching to play in the water. To explore all those fascinating planes and angles.

Slowly, head tilted back, he turned. Water ran in rivulets over hills and through valleys outlining the tightest six-pack she'd ever seen. Flat planes arrowed down past jeans that, stretched from a hard day's work, hung low on his hips. So. Low.

Julie licked her lips. Imagined lapping at the water, drinking her fill. She forced her gaze up toward the source of the water, pausing to admire his well-defined pecs. Just then, he shook his head, sending diamond droplets flying in a wide arc, breaking the trance she'd been in.

She blinked, and her gaze clashed with his. "Oh!" Her free hand flew to her mouth. Embarrassment heated her skin. Colin smiled wide then, with a wink, he turned, cranked the spigot off, and walked away without another look.

Julie yanked the curtain into place. "Damn him!" She stomped over, picked up the basket of dirty laundry, and clunked down the stairs. "Damn arrogant ass!"

She dropped the basket on top of the machine then grabbed the edge with both hands to steady herself. After a few deep breaths, she felt better, more in control. Forgetting all about the laundry, she grabbed a beer from the refrigerator and went to the front of the house—as far away from Colin Parker as she could get and still be indoors.

How long had he known she was there? A few minutes? Or had he known she'd been watching him all week?

She groaned and let her head fall against the sofa cushion, only to jerk it back up as the movement reminded her of the way he'd stood just moments before.

Would these new images ever go away?

"Not in this lifetime," she muttered.

God. Caught looking like a schoolgirl in the boys' locker room. How embarrassing.

Even worse, he knew!

He knew!

She couldn't do it again. No more peeking. "No more." She shook her head.

"No more," she confirmed.

❧

Colin smiled as he walked to his tent. Smiled as he gathered clean clothes. Smiled all the way to the stock tank. Smiled as he stripped out of his dirty clothes. Smiled as he walked in up to his knees then dove into the deeper water. He'd been pleasantly surprised to find out the tank was fed by a natural spring. The constant flow of fresh water kept the pond clean and the water cool even on the hottest of days, making it the perfect place to rinse off after a day of back-breaking work.

As he stepped out on the grassy bank and lay down to air dry, thoughts of his sexy neighbor once again came to mind. God, she was cute. She'd been watching him all week. Just a peek, now and then. But he'd known and let her have her fun. Thinking about her made his body react, and since the only person likely to find him out here was Julie—and she hadn't set foot on his property since the day he'd set up the tent—he saw no reason not to take the edge off. It had been too long since his dick had seen any action, and being close to Julie every day, knowing she was watching him and not being able to do a damn thing about it, was driving him bat-shit crazy. It was also one of the reasons he worked himself into the ground every day.

But today, just like every other day, as soon as he stopped working, his thoughts turned to her, and his body ached. He'd done a good job of ignoring it, but a man could only take so much, and Colin Parker had reached his limit.

With one arm serving as a pillow, he bent his knees, dug his heels into the soft earth, and stroked himself. Closing his eyes, he let his imagination run along the same path it did every night, and, soon, he was making love to Julie, her lithe body rising up to meet his as he drove into her wet heat over and over again. Imaginary lovers could never be as good as the real thing, but when he finally exploded, splashing ribbons of hot cum over sun-touched skin, he welcomed the relief.

He lay there, letting his heart rate return to normal, and wondered how much longer it would take to break through the wall Julie had erected between them. Remembering the first time he'd caught her peeking at him from an upstairs window, he smiled. She hadn't cut a door in the wall, but she was peeking over it. It wasn't much, but it *was* progress.

He just didn't know how much longer he could live like this. Wanting. Needing. Imagining what he couldn't have. Might never have. He'd thrown nearly every asset he had into the property next door to hers, and the idea of living so close to her yet so very far away was flat-out unacceptable.

His skin cooled as the sun dipped below the trees forming a living fence on the far side of the stock tank. Diving back in, he rinsed away the evidence of his lonely loving. Using the clean shirt he'd brought along as a towel, he dried himself off then pulled on his last clean pair of jeans. After donning a clean pair of socks and his work boots, he headed up the hill to his makeshift housing.

CHAPTER TWELVE

Invitations weren't his style, so he'd put the word out to a few friends, trusting them to spread the news about his little get-together tonight. There could be anywhere from two or three people who showed up or there might be two dozen. Or more. It didn't matter to him. He had a couple of packages of hot dog wieners and a couple of cases of beer. Everything else would take care of itself just as it had when he'd been in high school. He and his friends had gathered almost every weekend night on the shores of the local lake. Everyone knew to show up with a guitar and something to eat or drink. They'd all gone home, stomachs and hearts full to the brim. Tonight wouldn't be any different.

As the cars began to arrive and his backyard filled up with lawn chairs and picnic coolers, he kept an eye on the house next door, hoping to catch a glimpse of his neighbor. He'd spent most of the day outside, laying the last few pavers and tidying up the area. Mostly, he'd spent his time watching for the sexy brewmaster next door. Her dog had come over a couple of times, but Julie had remained out of sight.

He knew every one of the people gathered on his lawn, had known most of them his entire life. It was good to see them all again, but there was one person missing. If he could catch Julie looking out the window, he'd signal for her to join them. Then, the night would be perfect.

His friends didn't disappoint. Everyone brought something to share. Besides hot dogs cooked on the makeshift grill he'd made out of an old grill rack he'd found in the barn balanced on a couple of sticks of rebar stretched across the fire pit, they dined on homemade potato salad, fruit salad, chips and dip. Someone had picked up brownies from the diner out by the freeway, and another had brought homemade chocolate chip cookies. There was beer and wine for the adults, and those who'd brought the next generation with them provided age-appropriate drinks for them.

Colin made the rounds, paper plate in hand, spending a few minutes with each guest, getting to know the new additions—wives, husbands, and kids he'd missed meeting while he'd been in Nashville. He'd almost made the complete circuit when another pickup came up the driveway. All heads turned to see who the late arrival could be. Randy Tucker ambled around the corner of the house, a small cooler in one hand, a guitar case in the other.

Colin smiled. "Randy," he said, taking the insulated bag from him and setting it on top of his own cooler. "I didn't think you were going to come."

"Almost didn't."

Colin nodded at the case the man had in a white-knuckled grip. "You play?"

"A little. Don't know why I brought it." His gaze assessed the group gathered around the fire pit then returned to Colin. "I'm an amateur by your standards."

Colin chuckled as he clapped Tucker on the shoulder. "No worries. Some of these guys have been playing all their lives and still can't find a tune in a well bucket. Have you eaten?"

"Yeah."

"There are some damn good brownies around here somewhere." He looked around, found the person he wanted, and crooked his finger at her. "Chrissy. Come here, there's someone I want you to meet." She was the only female who'd come alone, and she'd set up camp next to him. They'd known each other forever, and because she played guitar as well as anyone he knew, she'd been part of his circle of friends as long as he could remember. They'd dated a few times in high school, but nothing had ever come of it.

The long-legged blonde stood and tossed her paper plate in Colin's solitary garbage can before joining them. "Hey," she said, giving Tucker the once-over.

"Hey," Tucker said.

"Randy, meet Chrissy Baxter. Chrissy, this is Randy Tucker. He's the restoration expert I hired to fix this place up. Tucker, Chrissy is an interior decorator by day but moonlights as a Dallas Cowboys Cheerleader. She also plays a mean six-string—unless she's lost her touch."

"I haven't lost anything, and the name is Christine." She glared at Colin then turned her star-powered smile on Tucker. "It's nice to meet someone who doesn't think I'm still six years old."

From the look on the restoration expert's face, he didn't think she was a child. Far from it. Nevertheless, Colin protested. "I don't think you're six. Sixteen, maybe."

"Shut up, Colin Parker, or I'll tell Mr. Tucker about the time you—"

"Whoa. Stop right there." Colin held his hand up. He knew where she was going with her comment and put a stop to it. That was the problem with people you'd shared a sandbox with. They knew things. Embarrassing things. "If I concede you're all grown up now, will you keep an eye on Randy for me?"

"Sure. Come on," she said, grabbing the guitar out of his hand. "I brought an extra chair."

Chrissy hadn't lost her touch. Her fingers flew over the guitar strings, keeping up with Colin and shaming most of the others. If anything, she'd improved since the last time he'd heard her play. How long had it been? Probably the night before high school graduation. They'd all gathered out at the lake for one last jam session. Some of his friends had gone off to college, others had taken jobs. A few had gotten married— thus the kids running around. Colin had loaded his battered suitcase and the guitar he'd made in woodshop in the pickup he'd bought with money he'd earned working odd jobs and hightailed it out of town like a posse was after him. He'd been halfway to Nashville before the ink dried on his diploma.

Someone threw another piece of scrap lumber on the fire. Sparks danced in the air, flickering out, ash floating down while all around, friends took turns choosing the song. Most knew them all and joined in. Others played the parts they knew or could pick up on. Everyone sang when they felt like it. No one criticized. Colin had honed his skill around campfires like this one, playing with friends who didn't care if he missed a note or changed the lyrics to suit himself.

He'd missed this in Nashville. Sure, he'd made friends and sat around playing music with them, but it hadn't been the same. There'd been an agenda lurking like a dirty river beneath every jam session. Professional jealousy came in many forms and could cut to the bone. He couldn't count the number of people he'd called friend who'd abandoned him the minute he'd achieved what they considered success. And for every one of them, there'd been two to take their place. People who wanted to be his friend. Some had hoped his success would rub off on them. Others had wanted to ride his coattails to the top. A few had wanted to sabotage his career. For what reason, he had no idea.

Then there had been the women. There'd been a time when having beautiful women throw themselves into his path would have made his day. But those last few months, there'd only been one woman on his mind. Glancing up at the window he knew gave her the best view of his property, he tried not to let his disappointment show.

Dammit. His impromptu show with the water hose had scared her off. Or, more likely, winking at her had done the trick. He shouldn't have let her know he had seen her. Doing so had given her one more reason to avoid him.

Suddenly weary, he strummed the last notes of the familiar country ballad then set his guitar aside. Others followed suit. Still others stood and stretched then began to pack up their belongings. Tomorrow was Monday, and most of them had jobs to get to. Wishing the night wasn't over but knowing it had to be, he raised his voice so everyone could hear him. "Thanks for coming out tonight. Same time next week?"

He'd never meant for the night to be anything but a one-time event, but the positive responses coming from his invitation made him smile. Once the construction was completed, he'd probably spend most days out here all alone, so the idea of making tonight a regular weekly event sounded like fun. He could already feel the creative juices that had all but dried up in Nashville beginning to flow again. A booster shot once a week could only be good for his career.

Waving goodbye to the last car to drive out, he tossed some more wood on the fire and picked up his guitar. It was late, but when his muse visited, he knew enough to listen to what it had to say.

∾

"You don't know what it's like." Julie sat at the giant marble-topped island in the center of Roseanne's new kitchen while her friend worked her magic with her new copper-clad coffee-making monster. The thing looked like it belonged in a high-end coffee shop, not someone's kitchen.

"I can imagine," Roseanne said as she set a mug filled with a delicious-looking concoction in front of Julie. "I've heard Colin play, remember? And I can imagine who shows up out there. We have some very good musicians in town. Some are amateurs only because they want to be."

Julie knew the statement to be true. The first week Colin had hosted his Sunday night jam session, she'd spent the evening wearing noise-cancelling headphones. The next week, she'd opened her bedroom window just enough to let the sound in. Last night, she'd moved an easy chair closer to the window and with the lights off, snuck a peek or two. "I'll give you that, but do they have to play every Sunday night? Don't these people have jobs?"

Roseanne chuckled as she set her beverage down and joined her friend at the island. "Most of them do, I suppose. What time did the hoedown break up last night?"

"Ten o'clock." Just as it had the previous two Sundays. She could live with everyone leaving at ten. It was what happened after that kept her awake. After his guests left, Colin sat outside and played all by himself. She didn't know what he was doing, but his clear bass voice carried, and, short of putting on the noise-cancelling headphones he'd given her, she couldn't help but hear.

"Ten doesn't sound so bad." Roseanne took a sip of the latte she'd fixed for herself. "If he has another one, you should go over."

Julie shuddered. "I don't sing or play. I'd be out of place."

"That's nonsense if I ever heard it. Colin wouldn't give a damn. And what's one more guest? You said everyone brings food to share. I'll make my coconut cake or a plate of double chocolate brownies for you to take. Throw in some of your newest brew, and trust me, no one there will care whether you can sing or play."

"There might not be a next time." *Liar.* She'd heard Colin extend the invitation just as he had the week before. For all she knew, it would turn into a regular thing, and she'd be sentenced to spending every Sunday evening for the rest of her life listening at the window.

"You know Colin would welcome you."

She hadn't exactly been the nicest neighbor since he'd pitched that ridiculous tent in his yard. "I don't know. I gave him heck about his tent."

"It's a tent. By definition it's temporary housing."

"I know, but you should see it. It's a good thing we're having a dry summer. If it rains, he's in big trouble."

"Don't look now, but trouble is on the way. Weather dude says we're in for a big storm sometime next week."

CHAPTER THIRTEEN

"He's nuts," she muttered to Bud who took up most of the floor space in her kitchen while she stepped around him to cook. "It's raining cats and dogs out there." And had been for most of the day. From her bedroom window, she had a bird's-eye view of Colin's yard. The place was a mud hole, and the roof of his tent was collecting rainwater in several places. Every now and then, he'd poke the sagging canvas from inside, sending water cascading off the roof. As she dropped a dirty spoon in the sink, her gaze drifted to the window. "Oh. My. Lord."

"Bud. You won't believe what he's doing now." She watched for a minute longer before she closed her eyes with a sigh. "I can't believe I'm going to do this."

Julie slipped on her mud boots and grabbed an umbrella. "Wait here, Bud. I'll be right back."

Colin joined her at the barbed-wire fence separating their properties. "What are you doing out here?"

"I came to ask you the same thing," Julie said. "Are you nuts? You can't cook in the rain."

"Sure you can," Colin said, though there wasn't much conviction in his words.

She motioned to the camp stove he'd set up on a set of sawhorses. One side had sunk into the mud, leaving the stove sitting at a precarious angle. How he thought he was going to cook on it, she didn't know. "Put that away and come over. I've got enough for two."

A few minutes later, Colin Parker arrived on her porch, soaked to the bone and carrying two plastic grocery bags. "Here," he said, handing her one of the bags. "My mama would tan my hide if I showed up for dinner without bringing something to share."

"You didn't— Oh!" She pulled the bottle of wine out and examined the label. Having tended bar, she recognized the winery, if not this specific wine. "You shouldn't have."

Colin held the other bag up. "Well, I was hoping your hospitality would extend to the use of your shower. I'm chilled to the bone."

He'd left his muddy boots in the mudroom, but the legs of his jeans were covered in black goop. Water dripped from his hair and shirt onto what had been a clean floor a few minutes ago. Now she understood the expensive wine. She closed her eyes again, praying for patience. When she opened them again, his eyes pleaded with her to take mercy on him.

"Okay, okay. But if you get mud all over my house, I'll leave you out in the rain next time." Julie turned to check on the meatloaf in the oven. "I've only got one bathroom. It's at the top of the stairs." She pointed to the staircase leading off the kitchen. "Towels are in the cabinet next to the vanity."

"Thank you. I won't leave a speck of mud anywhere. I promise."

Julie bent to look through the oven's glass panel. When she stood, the sight of long, hairy legs and a tight ass encased in white cotton briefs streaking through her kitchen almost caused her to drop the wine bottle she still held. Carefully setting the bottle down, she grasped the edge of the countertop with both hands, letting her head fall between her hunched shoulders. "Oh, God. What have I done?"

It's just dinner, she rationalized. *I can do this.* The old pipes groaned, confirming he'd found, and was using, her shower. Her mind automatically merged the images she'd stored of him working shirtless in his yard with the new image she had of his other half. She'd already seen him half-naked taking a shower from a water hose. It was a short leap from there to imagining him naked in *her* shower, water and ribbons of soapy suds cascading over the hard planes of his torso and the corded muscles of his legs.

Julie shook her head to dislodge the image her subconscious had conjured up. Lord, how many women would give anything to have Colin Parker naked in their shower? Millions, probably, which was all the reason she needed to bring herself down to earth. The plastic bag of clothes he'd brought with him was just a tip of the iceberg. The man had baggage. Lots and lots of baggage. She didn't need the kind of complications he brought with him. Having him as a neighbor was going to be bad enough. It was a done deal, though. He was moving in, already had if you counted the tent, and she wasn't going anywhere. Moving the brewery was out of the question. She'd given some thought to the logistics of their situation. Tonight would be the perfect time to discuss some of her concerns and ideas with her new neighbor.

He entered the kitchen just as she was dishing up the sliced meatloaf and whipped potatoes. She handed him a plate and motioned to the flatware drawer she'd left open. "Grab a fork. We can eat in here, if you don't mind?" One of the things she liked best about her house was the large eat-in kitchen. She'd had the dining room enclosed, and the space had become her office. She had a smaller one off the brewing room, but she ran the business out of her home office.

"Man, this looks and smells great," Colin said, taking a seat at the scarred table she'd picked up at an antique store. "Thanks."

Julie set her plate down across from Colin then headed for the refrigerator. "Something to drink? I have iced tea and beer."

"Beer sounds good."

She popped the tops on two unlabeled bottles, tossed the caps in a wastebasket sitting next to the refrigerator then joined Colin at the table. He turned the bottle a full turn. An eyebrow raised in question.

"It's a full-bodied ale for fall and winter," she told him. "I haven't named it yet."

"Am I the first to try it?"

"Besides me, yes. Let me know what you think."

The moment the rim of the bottle touched his lips, Julie's brain went into overdrive. Memories she'd tried so hard to suppress came rushing back. The feel of his lips on hers. The heat that had started with a spark and grown to a conflagration in a matter of seconds. Heart racing, she forced her gaze down to the plate she'd prepared for herself. She picked up her fork and dug into the mashed potatoes. How many times did she have to tell herself he wasn't *the one*? Hell, he wasn't even a contender. Colin Parker was a threat to the nice, quiet—safe—life she had worked so hard to build.

"Wow." Colin smacked his lips then raised the bottle for another taste. "This is fabulous."

"Thanks." She sipped from her own bottle. It was good. Probably one of the best she'd brewed yet. She could see making it a seasonal tradition if it sold as well as she thought it would. "Look, Colin, I've been thinking."

"About?" He took a bite of the meatloaf, humming his appreciation for the flavor.

"For starters, the fence. I'm thinking we should have something more substantial than we have now. Old barbed wire isn't much good for anything. What do you think? I'd be willing to pay for half of it."

"I've been thinking about our fence, too. We can't have you tearing your clothes on the barbs. I'm having horse fencing put up across the front of my property. I could ask them to extend it along our border, with a gate of course, so you and Bud can come and go as you please."

"Sounds like a good idea, but I was thinking of something a bit different. I'm sure you would like your privacy—"

Colin set his fork down and trained his gaze on her. "I like my privacy as much as the next guy, but also don't want to look at a brick wall when I'm in my backyard. If I'd wanted a damn wall I would have bought a place in town."

Julie set her fork down, too. She didn't know what had got his dander up. She'd only been trying to do the neighborly thing and allow him some privacy. "I'm not talking about a brick wall. Just a privacy fence. A six-footer should do it. And there's no need for a gate. Bud has plenty of room to roam over here."

The old wooden chair groaned as Colin straightened his shoulders and glared at her. "Horse fencing or nothing."

"Why are you being so stubborn? A privacy fence will give you peace of mind."

"It'll give me a headache."

"You're being ridiculous. You live next door to a brewery. A six-foot-tall fence will insulate you from my business and provide privacy for you. Isn't that why you bought the property?"

"I knew there was a brewery next door when I bought the property, and, yes, I was also looking for privacy, which I have. Some additional fencing along the front, along with an electronic gate, similar to the one you have at the road will ensure it." Colin pushed away from the table and stood. "Thanks for the shower and dinner."

Julie sat, rooted to her chair, as Colin stalked past her. What had seemed like a reasonable conversation had taken a sudden turn she struggled to comprehend. When her brain finally caught up, she bolted for the mudroom.

"Wait!" she called. But it was too late. Halfway to the fence that had caused so much trouble, his clothing was already soaked. "Dammit."

She slammed the door shut then leaned against it. Bud sat in the doorway between the mudroom and kitchen, watching the goings on with interest. "Stubborn ass." Bud woofed. Julie patted him on the head. "You and I are in agreement, Buddy. It will serve him right if he catches a cold."

Returning to the kitchen, she sat to finish her meal, but the nearly full plate across from her mocked her every bite. It was just a fence. With a gate. No need to get riled up about it. So why had they argued?

Appetite lost, she reexamined every word said since he'd come strolling into the kitchen in tight jeans and an I heart Nashville T-shirt and bare feet. His wet hair stood out in all directions, making her want to run her fingers through it—to tame it.

"This is ridiculous," she said. Bud's ears perked up, and his tail wagged. "I provoked him, Bud. It was either make him mad or jump his bones." Elbows propped on either side of her plate, she dropped her forehead into her upturned hands. Somewhere along the way, she'd convinced herself a wooden fence between them was the answer to her problem. Out of sight, out of mind. She could see it now for the sorry excuse it was. She'd tried to build a fence around her heart, and when the strategy hadn't worked, she'd come up with the idea of a fence between their properties. But deep in her heart, she knew a fence wouldn't work, either.

It was *The Kiss*. She'd wanted more from him then, and nothing had changed since. She still wanted Colin Parker. Wanted to feel the heat of his skin, run her fingers through his adorably mussed hair, feel his lips on hers, and so much more. *Down that road be dragons.* She raised her head, and her gaze landed on his unfinished meal. Her brain conjured up an image of his broad shoulders and firm ass, soaked to the bone, fleeing her house.

"Talk about dragons," she muttered. She'd shown her fangs and spit flames at him and quite possibly reduced the fragile bridge between them to cinders. All because she couldn't forget *The Kiss*. It had taken on a life of its own in the months he'd been gone. He'd admitted he should have taken it further instead of sending her off alone, but since his return he'd said nothing about wanting a relationship. He hadn't wanted one then, and he didn't want one now. Getting into the self-inspection, she had to admit the lack of interest on his part hurt. The man probably had dozens of women in Nashville throwing themselves at him. She'd been a distraction. Someone to pass the evening with after his sister's wedding. A way to amuse himself until he could get the heck out of Butte Plains.

He was back now, and her neighbor. It was time to get over *The Kiss*. Nothing could ever have come of it anyway. He was a paparazzi magnet, and she was camera shy—for good reason. Being seen with Colin Parker a few months ago hadn't carried any risk, but things were different now. He could put up an electronic gate and miles of horse fencing, but none of it would keep a determined photographer from taking pictures. Hadn't she just read about a Hollywood type who was suing a photographer for using a drone to take photos of him swimming in his own pool? No fence was going to protect Colin from a sophisticated privacy breech.

Neither one of them could stay behind their locked gates forever. Eventually, they had to come out, and Lord help her if they were together. Photos would be taken, and the safety she'd worked so hard for would be lost.

Colin's unfinished meal mocked her. Behind their locked gates, they could still be friends. Couldn't they? He'd been perfectly reasonable to propose the new horse fence to replace the rusty barbed wire. It would look nicer than a six-foot-tall privacy fence. And it was generous of him to allow Bud to continue romping across his property. He loved chasing the ducks at Colin's stock tank.

"I was an ass," she said to Bud. "Do you think I should apologize?" Bud barked once, voicing his approval. "Guess there's no time like the present."

CHAPTER FOURTEEN

Colin shed his wet clothes, tossed the sheet of plastic he used to keep his bedding dry onto the floor, and lay down. He'd been an ass. Why did he let her rile him so? "Goddammit." He brushed a drop of water from his forehead. She'd been right about the tent leaking, and he'd been right about her taking pity on him, though she'd only invited him in for a hot shower and a meal. *Fuck.* Out of dry clothes, he was cold, hungry, and miserable, and he had no one to blame but himself.

He'd seen the way she looked at him when he walked into the kitchen after showering. She'd wanted him, and he'd wanted her just as much, but he'd wanted a hot meal, too. The ginormous gas grill he'd ordered had been placed on backorder. He'd managed a few things on the fire pit, but if he never saw another hot dog or can of beans or, Heaven help him for saying it, steak again as long as he lived, he'd be happy. Damn, her meatloaf had been good, and the whipped potatoes to die for. But the most delectable thing at the table had been Julie.

Shit. She looked good enough to eat, and he'd planned on having her for dessert. He wasn't a Neanderthal. He knew women appreciated the buildup. Foreplay. And there was no better foreplay than sharing a meal together. He'd seen the way she watched his lips when he brought a bite to his mouth, and Lord knew he'd been watching her eat.

God, those lips. He'd never forget the way they felt beneath his, and, fuck, how many times had he imagined them wrapped around his dick? A million, at least. Every damn time he took himself in hand, for sure. It was his favorite fantasy, and one he'd practically worn out the last few months.

It was going to have to last him a lot longer. He'd let her talk about erecting an ugly privacy fence between their properties get to him. She was shutting him out, just like he'd shut her out when she'd come to see his tent. He should have known his behavior would come back to bite him in the butt, and damned if it didn't hurt like a son of a gun.

He closed his eyes and listened to the staccato sound of rain drumming down on the camp stove he'd left outside. There was a song in there somewhere. Something about loneliness or stupidly letting go of *the one* in order to pursue other goals only to find out later she didn't want you.

But she did. He wasn't a clueless teenager any longer. He'd had some experience with women. He knew when one wanted him, and, by God, Julie Davis had had that look in her eyes when he joined her in the kitchen. His horny subconscious hadn't imagined it. So, why all the talk about putting up fences? There wasn't a fence big enough to keep in the sound of his weekly jam sessions. Hell, she watched and listened from an upstairs window. One he now knew was in her bedroom.

No, she wanted to build a fence because she didn't *want* to want him.

Now, there was a song. A fucking sad song, to be sure.

He'd have to change her mind. How, he didn't know. Maybe it was a case of just having to wear her down. Dismantle the fence she'd put up between them, one picket at a time.

"Colin! Are you in there?"

He sat up, cursing as a drop of water meant for his forehead plopped on his shoulder and proceeded to roll down his bare chest. Fucking rain. He would have ditched the tent at the first sign of rain and bunked in his new old house tonight except the floors had just been refinished. The place stunk to high heavens, and stepping on the floors would be like stepping on a giant glue trap.

"Julie?" He reached for his wet jeans and struggled into them. He was trying to button the fly when she appeared on the other side of his duct tape-patched screen door. "Hey." He unzipped the panels to let her in. "What are you doing here?"

"You didn't finish your dinner." She held out a plastic container with one hand. With the other, she produced a bottle of beer from the pocket of her raincoat. "Peace offering?" Her gaze seemed to follow the path of the water droplet making its way along the same path as his happy trail.

Goddamn. She had that look again. He manhandled the top button through the hole in his waistband and mentally said, "Fuck it," to the rest of them. His dick was so hard, and the jeans too wet to make them work. "Thanks." He took her offerings and motioned for her to sit on the dry end of his cot. "I shouldn't have left the way I did. You were just trying to be a good neighbor."

"I wish that were true." She began to remove her coat.

"I wouldn't if I were you." He waved his hand holding the beer at the ceiling just as a big, fat drop of water let go of the canvas. It plopped right where his head had been a minute ago. "I can't vouch for the integrity of my ceiling."

She ditched the coat with a shrug. "I'll take my chances." She perched on the cot, her hands nervously skimming over her thighs. "I came to apologize. I don't know what got into me. I'm not usually rude to guests."

Colin removed the top on the plastic container. Inside was the meal he'd left behind and a set of plastic utensils. "I was the one being rude. As you said, you were just thinking of me, of my needs." As much as he wanted her meatloaf, he wanted her more.

"Again, I wish that were true." She watched as he brought a forkful of tasty meat to his lips. "But I was thinking of my own needs."

Colin jerked his gaze to hers. "I'd like to hear more about your needs." If that wasn't the cheesiest line ever delivered, he didn't know what was. Her cheeks turned an adorable shade of pink, and he couldn't help but wonder if he'd find the same shade in a more intimate part of her. His dick throbbed, making its needs known.

"You don't want to know. I mean, you didn't then. I can't imagine you would now."

Whoa. If not for the lump of meatloaf stuck in his throat, he would think this was a dream. But it wasn't. She looked as nervous as a cat in a room full of rocking chairs, but he admired her guts. Julie Davis wasn't a wilting daisy. Hell, no. She was a rose, thorny, but worth the risk, and damn if he hadn't already risked it all. His manager had warned him this move could be career suicide, but he'd done it anyway. Because of this woman. He set the container on top of the cooler/chair/table. Taking her face in his hands, he brushed his thumbs over her cheekbones. The heat of her blush made him want to feel the same heat surrounding his cock. "I'm sorry about the way we parted back then. You know—after my sister's wedding? I wanted you so much then it scared me. I've wanted you every day since. I want you now." He dragged one thumb over her lips. "It was more than just a kiss."

"Was it?" Her hot breath caressed his thumb.

"You know it was." His gaze dropped to her lips. "Should we give it another try?"

"Probably not." She swayed toward him. One hand landed on his chest, branding him while her lips parted in invitation.

"Probably not," he agreed, meeting her halfway.

Their lips touched, tentative at first, but the spark he remembered was still there, hot enough to ignite even the wettest timber into flame. When her hands snaked over his shoulders and speared through his hair, he took the kiss deeper—and sank into the fire. Need and want consumed him. He was toast, and though the realization should have scared him, it didn't. Not this time. Julie Davis was his.

When she moaned and pulled away from him, his heart crashed to his feet. "Too many clothes," she said. Seconds later, her tank top landed on the floor. Struck stupid by the sight of her breasts encased in snow-white lace, he didn't realize her dilemma until she cursed. "Fuck. I can't get this loose."

"No hurry." He cupped her breasts, amazed at how they fit so perfectly into his palms. "I'll help you with it in a minute." His gaze met hers. "I've dreamed of this moment for so long. Let me just look at you for a second."

"But—"

"Shh." He rubbed her nipples through the lace and smiled when they responded to his touch. "We'll get to it. I promise."

"I need—"

"I know, sweetheart. I need it, too, but there's no rush now. Is there?"

"Um," she moaned as he gently squeezed her mounds. "Do that again. Please."

Colin wrapped one arm around her to support her then dipped his head to her chest. His tongue played across one lace-covered nipple then the next before he selected one to graze his teeth over. Her fingernails dug into his scalp. "Oh. Oh, Colin." Her head fell back, her hair brushing across his hand. He nipped at the other nipple then soothed it with his tongue. She writhed in his embrace, thrusting her chest toward him, begging for more.

"I love lace, especially white lace," he said, palming her soft globes. "But it's time for this to go."

With practiced fingers, he worked the back closure loose. "Keep your hands right where they are." He drew first one strap then the other over her shoulders and down to the crook of her arms so her bra hung between them like clothes on a line. He liked the feel of the lace against his skin, but the view was better this way. Her rose-tipped breasts were high and firm. His prior examination had assured him they were the real thing. Artificial wouldn't have been a deal breaker, but he was damn glad they weren't. He cupped her right breast, brought it to his mouth, and licked the rosy tip. When he blew on the wet flesh, it drew up tight and hard. Shit, she was beautiful, and he said so. "You are so fucking beautiful. I could do this all day." To prove his point, he applied his tongue to her left breast then blew on it, too.

"Colin." His name, spoken like a plea confirmed it was time to move on. She needed more, and Heaven knew, he needed all of her.

"Lie down, sweetheart. You are definitely wearing too many clothes."

Her hands slipped from his head to his shoulders then trailed down his chest as he lowered her to the foot of the cot, where hopefully, the roof would hold and not drench them both, though no amount of water was going to put out the fire burning inside him. "Hurry, Colin."

The tight, knit pants she wore hugged her calves and ended just above her ankles. He dug his fingers in under the waistband and tugged. Julie wiggled her ass and down they went, revealing a band of white lace that spanned her hips and dipped between her legs.

"Good God Almighty. Are you trying to kill me?"

She kicked her legs free of the pants then her gaze followed his. "They're just panties." Her thumbs hooked the sides. Colin covered her hands with his.

"No. Leave them on."

"They're in the way."

"No, they aren't." He pulled her hands free. "Hands above your head, sweetheart. Don't move them until I tell you to."

His tone brooked no argument, and she did as he said, but not without protest. "Bossy much?"

"Only when it comes to your pleasure." *And mine*, he thought as he bent over her. He pressed his nose to her crotch and inhaled. Damn, there couldn't be a more intoxicating scent. He couldn't wait to taste her, but there was plenty of time. In the gray light of dusk, she looked like an offering from the gods, spread across a cot that should have been a magnificent bed to match her beauty. *Next time*, he vowed to himself. Next time they'd have a soft mattress and pillows, and every luxury, but for now, this would have to do.

She lifted her hips, and he dug his chin into her pubic bone. "What did I say? There's no hurry, sweetheart."

"God, Colin, you're killing me."

"One kiss at a time," he said, placing a kiss along the top edge of lace. "One kiss at a time."

CHAPTER FIFTEEN

She was dying. Hands clasped above her head, she lay spread before him, and all he wanted to do was kiss her. His lips seared her skin as he worked his way across her belly, first one way then the other before dropping lower and doing it all over again. If he didn't get to her aching center soon, she was going to grab him by the hair and smother him with her pussy.

Each time she protested, he pressed her thighs wider, his callused fingertips sending shivers of need through her system. When he finally kissed his way to the crown jewel of her sex, she begged for mercy. "Please, Colin. I need you."

"I know, baby. I know." His hot breath fanned the flames of her desire, and she lifted her hips, seeking a satisfaction she feared only this man could provide.

Then his lips were on her through the lace of her panties. His tongue flicked at her clit, and she saw stars. Not an orgasm, but damn close. She moaned her frustration and urged him on with a pump of her hips.

"So beautiful." He breathed the words across her heated core then his tongue grazed her covered slit from bottom to top. "And, oh, so good. I need to taste you, sweetheart."

"Please, Colin. Oh, God, please!"

He pulled the lace down to her thighs then lifted one leg in order to slip the panties off, leaving them hanging from the other leg. She didn't care about the panties. All she cared about was feeling his lips on her, finding the pleasure his kisses had promised. She didn't have long to wait. He pressed her legs wide, opening her to his gaze. "Fucking beautiful," were the only words he spoke before his open mouth covered her.

Dear Lord! His lips and tongue were everywhere from her clit to her pussy and even to the place she'd always thought forbidden. But nothing was forbidden with Colin. It all felt good. No, better than good. The scruff of his beard against her sensitive skin added to her pleasure as he nipped and sucked and licked at her. She couldn't remain still, and he didn't stop her as she sought her pleasure, fucking his face.

His tongue teased her, dipped inside then flicked out to dance attendance on her clit before he closed his lips around the nub and sucked. Julie thrashed on the cot, making the old wooden frame creak and groan beneath her. Rain drummed on the canvas above them, a soundtrack to the storm brewing inside her. She was so close. So close. "Colin." She begged for something she couldn't name. A need unfulfilled.

Then he speared her with two fingers and she was even closer to the great unknown. She whimpered her need, and his fingers began to move. In. Out. In. Out. Gentle then harder. And harder. Faster. His teeth grazed her nub. She shattered as the most powerful orgasm she'd ever had tossed her on wave after wave of pleasure, and all the while Colin placed open-mouth kisses on her mound, her clit, her thighs. When, at last, she lay weak and spent on the cot, her breathing ragged, he slipped his fingers from her. She tried to clamp her legs closed, to hold him inside her, but his shoulders kept her open to him.

"That was the most beautiful thing I've ever seen," he said, the reverence in his tone, convincing. "I need to be inside you."

"Yes. Hurry, please."

"I need a raincoat—a condom," he clarified.

"I know what a raincoat is," she said. "Just hurry the fuck up. I'm freezing."

Colin rocked back on his heels as his right hand went to the pocket of his jeans where he kept his wallet. "Shit." Had it fallen out? He looked around on the floor, shoved his boots out of the way. Still nothing. Then it hit him. "Fuck!"

"What's the matter?" Goose bumps had formed on her delectable flesh, and her nipples were hard and turning purple in the cool moist air.

"My wallet is in the jeans I left at your house."

"I'll bring it to you tomorrow." The annoyance in her voice gave way to a gasp as she realized what his missing wallet meant. "Oh."

"Yeah, oh." Colin rubbed both hands over his face, forcing his libido into submission. He knew he was clean, and couldn't imagine she wouldn't be, but there were other things to consider, and he didn't take chances.

Julie scooted back on the cot enough so she could sit up. With one arm wrapped tight around her shivering torso, she used the other to push her hair out of her face. "Let's go." She reached for the waterproof jacket she'd worn earlier.

Still fighting the lust gripping him tight, it took a few seconds for Colin to register her meaning. "You want to go to your place? And—"

"Don't you want to?"

"Hell, yes. I just thought…"

"Don't think too much or I might change my mind."

At her words, his big brain shut off and his little brain took over. He helped her into her jacket then gathered up her clothes, stuffed them in a plastic grocery bag which he tucked under his arm, and ushered her out into the dark rainy night. The light above her porch acted as their beacon. He held the barbed wire while she climbed through before following.

117

Safely inside, she hung her wet jacket on a peg in the mudroom then, stark naked, padded over to the stacked washer and dryer on the other side of the small room. When she bent to retrieve his muddy jeans from a laundry basket, his heart pumped another liter of blood to his groin. Damn, she was going to be the death of him, but God, what a way to go!

"Here." Turning, she held his wallet out to him. His gaze swept over her beauty, pausing briefly on the neat patch of curls at the juncture of her thighs then again on her still-erect nipples. "Are we good?"

"Huh?" She waved the wallet under his nose. "Oh, yeah. Thanks." He prayed he had a condom in there. He could still remember his dad's voice asking him if he had protection before he went out on a date, and in the same breath admonishing him to think before he used it.

He eyed the small packet nestled between two twenty-dollar bills and breathed a sigh of relief. The voice of reason smacked him upside the head. Did he really want to use it? There was only one answer to his question. Hell, yes. He'd never wanted to use it more than he did right that second. He held the condom up. "I've only got one. Let's see how long we can make it last."

"Last one in bed is a rotten egg." Julie took off running. Colin did his best to keep up, but his hard-on crammed into wet jeans restricted his movement. When he shut her bedroom door behind him to keep Bud out, she was already tucked under the covers. "Do not bring those wet clothes into my bed."

"Wouldn't dream of it," he said, tossing the condom to her. "Hang onto that, will ya?"

Julie scooped it up from where it fell on the bed beside her then her gaze returned to him. Colin unbuttoned the one button he'd managed to fasten when she'd called out to him earlier. At the sight of his tighty-whities, she licked her lips. His dick twitched in anticipation of having those lips wrapped around it. Maybe later, after they'd used his one condom, he thought. Then they'd have to get creative.

"Want to see more?" he asked.

"Yes, please."

Her brazen answer pleased him. She knew what she wanted and wasn't afraid to ask for it. If she'd spoken up all those months ago, he wasn't sure he would have had the strength to send her home the way he did. Then again, he wouldn't be the person he was today if he'd stayed in Butte Plains. Shaking off thoughts of the past like raindrops, he hooked his thumbs under the waistband of his briefs and pushed them and the jeans past his hips to his thighs. His cock sprang free. The appreciation in her eyes was like throwing gasoline on a match. His restraint went up in flames.

Colin kicked his jeans and briefs off in record time then dove beneath the covers with her. She snuggled up to him, her ice-cold hands a welcome shock that allowed him a brief moment to think. "I want you so bad I don't think slow is going to be possible."

"We can do slow later," she said as her hand found his dick under the covers.

He grabbed her wrist just as she closed her fingers around him. "This is likely to be over before it begins if you follow through."

"That bad, huh?"

"Sweetheart, you have no idea."

"Then you'd better get this on." She held up the condom.

He snatched the packet out of her hand and kicked the covers down so he could see. He had only one chance to do it right. Any mistake and the party would be over. For the first time ever, his hands shook as he ripped the foil, thankfully leaving the contents intact. Rolling it on was sheer torture as every touch activated nerve endings already on edge. Suited up at last, he pulled the covers up over them and reached for her. Their lips met in a kiss that heated his blood as their tongues dueled. He moved so she was beneath him and settled between her legs, his cock pressed into her stomach. God, she was soft. His hands roamed, learning every inch of her. He couldn't get enough of her curves. Breaking the kiss, he tasted his way down her neck to her shoulder then down her chest to the swell of her breasts.

"Colin." He loved hearing his name on her lips, especially when she said it all breathless with a hint of impatience.

"Let me love you, sweetheart." He closed his lips around one nipple while his fingers teased at the other one. She cradled his head in her hands and arched into him. Lord, she tasted sweet. He switched breasts, lavishing attention on the other one the way he had the first. Her fingers played through his hair then closed into fists. When she tugged, he released her nipple.

"Oww!" he cried out playfully. "Too much?"

"Can we...can you...*now?*"

"I thought you'd never ask." He shifted so the head of his cock slid between her folds and nestled at her entrance. He could feel her wet heat through the thin latex barrier and, for the first time ever, wished the condom wasn't necessary. Colin planted his hands on either side of her, angling his body so he could see her face as he entered her. Instinctively, she brought her knees up, opening herself to him, and, in that moment, he pressed forward until her soft tissues caressed the head of his cock.

"Oh," she breathed. "You feel so good."

The strain of trying to go slow, to give her time to adjust to his size was eating away at his sanity. He counted to ten in his head then gave her another inch. His cock twitched and his balls drew up tight against his body. Shit. He was going to come and he hadn't even done anything. He wasn't going to last a minute at this rate. "Look at me, sweetheart."

When she opened her eyes, he mustered every ounce of self-control he had and said, "You feel too good, baby. I'm not going to last long."

She nodded. Her tongue darted out to wet her lips, and he almost lost it. He'd had more control than this when he'd been a virgin and Cindy Holcomb had laid on the bench seat of his old pickup and hiked up her skirt to reveal her bare snatch. He'd nearly driven off the road then recovered enough to drive to a secluded spot. It was the first time he'd used the condom in his wallet. The whole thing had lasted less time than it took for the radio DJ to play a Top 40 hit. Here he was, over a decade later, and he was going to come before Julie even took all of him.

"I want to feel you, all of you, inside me. I don't care how long you last, just let me feel you."

Her plea did nothing to ease the need clawing at him, but hearing her voice helped him focus on her pleasure rather than his. He'd make this good for her even if it killed him. "Eyes on mine," he said. When their gazes locked, he inched slowly forward until he was fully seated inside her welcoming body.

"Good God Almighty," he whispered. "You feel so good." Every cell in his body called for him to move, to pull out and thrust back in, over and over again, but as good as doing so would feel, it would be the beginning of the end, and he never wanted this to be over.

"You feel good, too." She wiggled her hips, and he saw stars.

"Don't, baby. Don't move." He could feel sweat beading on his forehead as he kept his need to move in check. "You'll make me come."

"Really? I could do that?"

"Easily," he said through his clenched jaw. Colin closed his eyes and concentrated on his breathing. *In. Out. No! Shit.* His entire body shook from the effort it took to remain still and just feel the wonder of being connected to Julie in this most intimate of ways. He'd never felt anything like it. He didn't want to move, but he had to. *Had to.*

Pulling out until only the tip remained inside her, he slid into her welcoming heat, and, once again, held himself still. "So good, baby. You feel so damn good."

"I need you to move, Colin. Please. It feels so good, but I need—"

"Me, too, baby. Me, too." Drawing their pleasure out wasn't going to happen. He'd given the effort everything he had and failed. It was time to let go. Time to give in to his desires. His hips rose and fell in a rhythm as old as time, driving him closer to release with each repetition. Not wanting to go over the edge without her, he reached between them. He knew he'd found the right spot to massage when her back bowed and she pressed her head into the pillow, exposing her lovely neck to him. Colin bent to trace the column from chin to the hollow at the base.

"Come for me, baby."

"Colin," she breathed.

"It's okay, baby. I've got you. Let go."

"Oh. Oh!"

Colin kissed his way around to the long-corded muscle running from her jaw to her shoulder. "Give it to me, baby."

He scraped his teeth across her skin then opened wide and clamped his teeth gently on her neck. Julie's body tensed then she flew apart, her hips bucking, her inner muscles convulsing around his cock. He buried his face in the crook of her neck, trying to hold on to his last measure of control, but the guttural sounds she made, and the way her fingers dug into his ass as she came shredded his intentions. Holding her tight, he lost the battle he'd been waging and gave in to his most basic and primal urges. His hips jerked, no sign of the rhythm he'd built his life around, and, with a cry from deep within, he came harder than he'd ever come in his life.

CHAPTER SIXTEEN

As sanity returned, Julie took a quick inventory. After an explosive orgasm, Colin's cock still felt warm and solid inside her like the last piece of a puzzle. The contrast between his skin and hers felt right, even if he was heavy. She let her legs and arms slide down to the cool sheet. When he rolled off her, she clamped her legs shut to ease the ache of loss there. He wasn't her first, but it was definitely the first time she'd felt so empty afterwards.

Without a word, Colin climbed off the far side of the bed. She admired his naked ass as he made his way to the en suite bathroom and closed the door. While water ran, she pulled the covers up over her and closed her eyes, trying to commit the last few minutes to memory. Who knew if or when they'd do it again, and how could it possibly be as good the next time? She didn't have much experience to compare with, but she had enough to know what she'd felt this time was different. More. Better. Life changing. She almost, *almost*, didn't want to try it again, certain a repeat performance wouldn't live up to the original. But, hey, even if it fell short, it would still be spectacular.

Hearing the doorknob turn, she turned her gaze to the door. Would he dress and leave, or join her in bed even though they'd used the only condom they had?

"Mind if I stay here tonight?"

"After what we just did? I'd be a damned ungrateful bitch to turn you out into the rain, wouldn't I?"

Colin grinned as he dove beneath the covers and pulled her close. "Yes, you would." He kissed her lightly on the mouth. "You were incredible. I'm sorry I didn't last longer."

"Don't apologize, please. I had two of the best orgasms ever. No complaints here."

"I aim to please," he said, rolling to his back and taking her with him so she lay on her side, her head resting on his shoulder. His callused fingers stroked her arm as he spoke.

"Like I said, no complaints."

"I'll go into town tomorrow and get more condoms."

"I didn't say it was good enough to repeat, did I?" she teased.

"What? Are you crazy?"

Julie giggled at his outrage. She ran her hand through the light hair on his chest that had felt so good as it rubbed against her nipples. "You want to do it again?"

"Hell, yeah. Don't you?"

"Yes. I'd like that very much."

"Then it's settled." He squeezed her tight in his embrace. "I sure wish I brought more condoms with me, but, after the way we parted last time I was here, I wasn't sure you'd let me in your bed."

"I wanted you then," she confessed.

"I wanted you, too, but—" Colin sighed. "I was scared."

"Of me?"

"No. Yes." His body grew tense. She waited for him to continue, to explain why he'd left the way he did. At last, he took a deep breath and let it out. "I was afraid if I made love to you, I'd never go back to Nashville, and I had to return. I'd invested too much in building my career to let it slip away. I knew I was taking a chance I might regret later, and I did regret it, every day, but I had no choice. I couldn't come home to Butte Plains a washed-up country singer wannabe. What would I do? Work the assembly line at my sister's sex toy plant? I would have hated my life, and I would have made you miserable in the process."

"I wish you'd told me why then. I was dazed and confused and horny. I even turned the wrong way out of the parking lot and had to double back in order to get home. When I did get home and had time to think about what you'd done, I got mad. Were your ears burning?" she asked with a smile. "I think I called you every name I could think of then started making up new ones."

Colin rubbed one ear. "That's what was wrong! I thought I'd gotten an ear infection or something. Darn near went to the doctor, but it cleared up on its own."

"Eventually, I chalked it up to experiences best not repeated, and the name-calling stopped."

"Until I showed up at the tasting room, looking for you. I could swear my ears were getting a workout then."

"Nope. Must have been someone else calling you names." She tried to hide her amusement, but it spilled out in waves of laughter.

"It was you, then." Colin rolled her beneath him and began to tickle her ribs. Before long, he was kissing her, and his hands gentled, seeking out her most intimate places. "I can't get enough of you," he said as he pushed two fingers into her slick opening.

Julie spread her legs wide for him then dug her nails into his shoulders as his touch ignited a desire she'd thought quenched by their earlier lovemaking. "God, that feels good," she moaned.

"This time, it's all for you, baby. Just relax and let me make you come."

His cock, hard and heavy pressed into her thigh. She wanted him inside her but knew they had to be reasonable—take precautions. With no plans to enter into any kind of relationship, she'd quit taking the pill when she moved to Butte Plains, and Heaven only knew who he'd been with. She refused to think about all the women in Colin's life. Right now, she was the only one in his bed—well, her bed—and nothing else mattered. Especially when he was doing such wonderful things to her body.

With his free hand, he palmed her breast then teased the nipple to a hard peak before taking it into his mouth. Flames engulfed her from the inside out as he licked and tugged on the sensitive bud while, below, his talented fingers stroked and strummed until she began the familiar climb to the top of the cliff. His teeth grazed her nipple at the same time his thumb flicked her clit. It was not enough and too much at the same time. She didn't even try to stop herself from falling from the cliff. Then she was flying through space, grasping for anything to anchor her to earth.

"That's it, baby. Come for me."

"Colin," she gasped as pleasure gripped her body.

❧

Could a guy die from blue balls? He was about to find out.

Watching Julie fly apart under his hands was one of the great wonders of his life and one he wouldn't trade for anything—even a cure for blue balls. He'd gladly suffer for her pleasure. As her body relaxed, he withdrew his fingers from her snug channel then rolled to his back, taking her with him. He managed to pull the covers up over them then tried to focus on the woman wrapped around him instead of his throbbing cock. No one had ever called him a selfish lover, and he would be damned if he was going to turn into one now. Julie was spent. Once she was asleep, he'd take a cold shower. Then he'd buy the biggest box of condoms he could find tomorrow, so this wouldn't happen again.

"That was amazing." Her warm breath on his skin combined with her soft curves pressed up against him almost sent him into orbit. "Thank you."

"Anytime, sweetheart. Anytime." He meant it. He'd be her booty call 24/7.

She raised up on one elbow, as she placed her hand on his chest her hair brushed his skin, sending shock waves through his body. "But what about you? It hardly seems fair."

"Don't worry about me."

Her fingers played through the smattering of hair on his chest then tracked lower, following the trail to his happy place.

"Careful." He grabbed her wrist, stopping her before she could wrap her hand around his boner.

"I could do something to help." Her fingers, stopped but not trapped, danced across his abdomen.

Colin groaned and clenched his jaw. "I'll be okay. You should get some sleep."

"Sleep is overrated." Escaping his grasp, she took his shaft in hand.

It was all he could do not to come immediately like some green kid getting his first hand job in the back seat.

"You're so hard." She worked her hand up and down his length. "Does it hurt?"

"In the best possible way," he replied through gritted teeth. His focus entirely on one part of his anatomy and what she was doing to it, he barely registered the cooler air brushing over his body when she kicked the covers off.

"I want to taste you. May I?"

"What? Huh?" He forced his eyes open. She wasn't where he thought she was. It took only a moment to see she'd shifted down the mattress so her face was even with his groin. *God almighty.*

"May I?"

"May you what?"

"Taste you." She pumped him once, twice.

Colin fought through a fog of need to make sense of her words. When his brain finally figured it out, he choked out a response. "God, yes." Then her lips were on him, sliding down his length, engulfing him in a hot, wet heaven. "Jesus, woman!" He rose to his elbows. No way was he going to miss seeing this.

Her fingers were wrapped around the root of his shaft, her rosy lips stretched tight as she worked her mouth up and down. Slowly. Colin sucked in a breath and held it until his lungs burned before he let it out in measured increments synced to her pace. At this rate, he was going to pass out either from lack of oxygen or from overstimulation. Christ, he couldn't watch and feel at the same time, not and survive. If he had to choose one, he chose feeling. Closing his eyes, he dropped back to the mattress and let her take him to paradise.

It was a short trip. He'd been halfway there before she even touched him. It had been a fast climb to the precipice from there. In minutes, an oath exploded from his lips at the same time he came against the back of her throat.

Colin clamped a hand over his chest, grateful to feel his heart still beating beneath his palm. "I thought I'd died and gone to Heaven," he said, only half joking. For a second, he'd thought he'd seen the pearly gates beckoning him home.

Julie crawled up and cuddled against his side. "I did it right, then?"

He chuckled. "Sweetheart, if you'd done it any more right you'd be calling 9-1-1."

"Think you can sleep now?"

"Hell, yeah. How about you?"

His answer was a light snore. It took some doing, but he managed to pull the covers up without disturbing her. Colin closed his eyes, and, in seconds, he was asleep.

CHAPTER SEVENTEEN

Julie woke, slightly disoriented. Colin Parker lay sprawled across her queen-sized bed, his hair mussed and his cheeks scruffy. He was sexy and adorable at the same time. She quickly decided it was a lethal combination and spelled the death of her regular schedule if she didn't move soon. A whimper outside the door was the catalyst that propelled her up and to the bathroom. She took care of business, donned a robe then eased out of the bedroom. Bud nudged her hand with his wet nose.

"Hi, Budster. You need to go out?" The dog wagged his tail and headed down the stairs. Julie followed, wincing as rarely used muscles complained of last night's activities. She let Bud out, scooped some kibble into his bowl then popped a pod in the coffee maker. It was unusual for her to have more than one cup in the morning, but this morning she wished she had one of those pods capable of producing a whole pot. If Colin stuck around, she'd have to pick some of those up at the store. And, find the carafe that had come with the machine. It was…somewhere.

She let Bud in and was checking her emails on her phone and working on her second cup of coffee when Colin came downstairs. He'd pulled on the only clothes he had upstairs, the jeans he'd worn to get from his tent to her house in the rain. She tried not to stare at his bare chest, but how could she not? Wide shoulders tapered to a trim waist and slim hips that fit perfectly between her legs. He was all hard muscle and golden tan skin her fingers itched to touch. Touching would lead to other things, which brought about another realization. They'd used the only condom they had last night. Which had led to other things. Her cheeks heated as she recalled how exciting those *other things* had been.

"Good morning." He crossed the room and bent to kiss her lightly on the lips. "You taste like coffee."

Julie forced her lascivious thoughts away and stood. "Want some?" She headed for the coffee maker. "It takes about thirty seconds."

"Please," he said, rubbing the dog's ears. "Has he been out?"

"Yep, and fed." Geez, they sounded like an old married couple. Julie's heart did a flip-flop. What the hell was she thinking? It was one night. One spectacular night, but still. She handed Colin the filled cup then resumed her seat at the kitchen table. He took the chair across from her and sipped the hot beverage. She guessed he wasn't much of a morning person. It wasn't a deal breaker, but it was a reminder of how little they knew about each other.

"What have you got planned today?" she asked.

He nodded at the window where bright sunlight streamed in. "Looks like a good day to work on the landscaping." His gaze went to the vintage cat clock on the wall above her head. "I've got a guy coming out this morning—finally—to give me an estimate on an electronic gate."

"Time for breakfast?"

Colin shook his head. "Nope. I'll grab a power bar. He's supposed to be here soon." He stood, drained the last of his coffee then set the cup in the sink. "Thanks, though. Another time?" His smile and the wicked sparkle in his eyes told her how much he'd like a repeat.

"Rain check?"

He groaned. "Please don't talk to me about rain. I'm up to my ears in mud as it is." He took her in his arms and drew her close. "But, yeah, I'll take a rain check."

His kiss stole her breath then he pulled away. She followed him to the door. Standing on the second step, he held the glass storm door open and leaned in for another kiss. Then he was gone, loping across her yard, dodging puddles. She watched until he put one hand on the top of a fence post and propelled himself to the other side. Closing the door, she leaned against it for a moment as memories of the night before flitted through her mind. If she had a brain in her head, she'd tell Colin Parker to get lost. To never come darken her door again. But, apparently, she'd lost her marbles because she had no intention of telling him any of those things.

ؘ؈؞

Colin couldn't wipe the smile off his face as he vaulted over the fence and crossed the yard to his tent. In the sunshine, the relic didn't look so bad, and truth, after last night, it would forever hold a special place in his heart. In his haste to get to Julie's place, and find his only condom, he'd left the front flap unzipped. He saw the fresh muddy footprints on the floor first. With all the rain yesterday, there was plenty of mud inside, but most of it had dried, and the prints he was seeing now were not his.

Maybe one of the workers had come looking for him? That was probably it. Shrugging it off, he went in search of the only clean T-shirt he had left. His sister had given it to him a few weeks ago when he'd taken her out to lunch. It was sold exclusively at their sex toy outlet store and bore a screen-printed photograph of the actual Butte Plains city limits sign. Shortly after Becky and Ford's success with their Backdoor Locking System butt plug, some ingenious person had modified the freeway marker to read Butt Plug city limits. In the photo memorialized on the shirt, they'd also added the word assholes beneath the Population 3469. The highway department had been quick to remove the qualifying word in regards to the inhabitants, and, thankfully, whoever had added it had not seen fit to do it again.

However, it didn't matter how many times they fixed the name of the city, within hours it would be modified again. They'd eventually given up, it seemed, and people on the interstate regularly passed through Butt Plug, Texas.

Colin found the shirt in one of the plastic bins he used to hold his meager food supplies. He considered turning it inside out but figured everyone had seen the sign, so what would it matter. He was out of clean socks, so he put on the least nasty ones he could find then slipped his feet into his boots. Intending to make use of his sister's washer and dryer when he went to town, he stuffed his dirty clothes into a garbage bag and set it next to the entrance. Heck, he could probably score a box of condoms from his sister—wait—he'd ask Ford instead. Getting sex supplies from his sister was too weird to contemplate, even if selling the stuff had made her a millionaire. Thinking of all the other interesting things he might score from his brother-in-law, he exited the tent with a smile on his face.

Would Julie like to experiment with some of the stuff his sister sold? Hell, he'd bet she already had one of their fancy vibrators. They were so popular, they'd even made the national news when they came out.

Colin shook his head. Who would've thought? He was chuckling and smiling to himself when he rounded the corner of the house and came face-to-face with a man he didn't recognize. His first thought was it had to be the gate contractor, but there was something about the way the man dressed that put Colin on alert. "Who are you?" he asked, not caring if he sounded friendly or not.

"So, you are living in a tent," the man said, which pretty much guaranteed he wasn't the man Colin was expecting.

"I said, who are you?"

"Just an interested party." His gaze darted over Colin's shoulder to Julie's house. "A little too wet for you last night? Or just wet enough?"

Every muscle in his body tensed. How long had this scum been hanging around? Had he seen him leave Julie's house? Damn paparazzi. "You're trespassing." He'd put signs up on the gateposts and every other fence post along the road frontage. The man had to have seen them. Colin retrieved his cell phone from his back pocket. "You've got thirty seconds to get off my property before I call the police."

"Hold your horses. I'm going." He took a few steps toward the empty driveway then stopped and turned to face Colin. "Nice shirt, by the way. I'll see you around."

Colin pocketed his phone as he watched the intruder saunter down the empty driveway. He must have walked from the road, which meant he could have been snooping around for hours. *Shit.* He hadn't seen a camera, but everyone with a cell phone these days had one.

Where was the gate guy? Hell, would a gate even keep the scum out? Maybe he needed to rethink his security measures. He'd once thought any publicity was good publicity, but not since the celebrity rags had started making up stories to go with the photos they snapped. He'd been romantically linked to women he'd only spoken to for a minute or two at a social event and broken up with more women than he'd actually dated. Heaven only knew what they'd make of him living in a tent. He could see the headlines now—*Country Star Colin Parker—Broke, Homeless, and Living in a Tent!* They'd make no mention of the house, clearly under construction. No. That might actually make sense. No story there.

So, maybe the tent was a bit extreme, but it worked for him on two levels. It kept him near the construction zone, and it had garnered some sympathy from Julie. She was talking to him now, and more, which was all good in his book. Still, he needed to call his publicist and give him a head's-up. Maybe he could get something out there to explain the tent like—*Colin Parker Communes with Nature on Camping Trip.* Yeah, that sounded good. He'd wait and call at a decent hour. No need to roust Cameron out of bed yet. The situation only existed in Colin's mind—at the moment.

Hearing the faint sound of a car starting, Colin gave the departing scumbag a one-finger wave goodbye then climbed the newly built steps to his house. If last night's humidity hadn't messed up the dry time for the floors, he should be able to walk on them this morning. He liked to walk through the house before everyone got there. He wasn't checking up on them—just getting a feel for his new living space. It was already beginning to feel like home, which was a good thing, wasn't it?

Thankfully, the floors were dry, but the smell of stain and polyurethane remained, so he went through the house, opening every window. He was standing at the window in what would be the master bedroom, looking out at the property next door, when Julie appeared on the pathway leading from her house to the brewing room. Bud ambled beside her, looking as if he'd made the trip a thousand times and was bored with it. If there wasn't so much going on over here during the day, he'd gladly let the Labrador retriever hang out with him.

The sound of multiple trucks coming up his drive drew his attention away from the window and what was rapidly becoming his favorite subject, Julie Davis. Hustling down the stairs, he greeted the men, and one woman, Emma, who he was told was one of the finest wood carvers in the state of Texas. They went right to work while Colin went to what would be his kitchen. Devoid of cabinets or appliances, they'd set a piece of plywood across sawhorses as a makeshift countertop. Colin plugged in the coffee maker he'd purchased from a local thrift store for a buck, filled its tank with water from a gallon jug then tossed the old filter, and put in a new one. As he scooped grounds, he thought about Julie's coffee maker and wondered what the next generation would think of this pot in a few years?

He snapped a picture of the appliance with his phone and posted it to his Instagram account with #oldschool.

Pouring the first cup for himself, he smiled at the sounds of progress going on throughout the house. Nail guns. Saws. Someone had turned on a radio, and country music filled the silence in between. Maybe he *was* old school. He liked the craftsmanship of days gone by. He liked pouring coffee from a glass carafe. Liked smelling it as it aged on the hot plate like fine whiskey in an oak barrel. Hell, he'd bet somewhere someone was working on a single pod thingy-jig for alcohol. Aged in plastic. He'd have to ask Julie what she thought of the idea in regards to beer. Everything was evolving. Even country music.

When it came to country music, he was definitely old school. He didn't much care for the so-called crossover tunes that straddled the fence between country and pop music. He was country all the way, and, so far, he couldn't complain. He'd done well singing his style of music. Seems there were still people out there who shared his views, and, as long as there were, he planned to keep writing and singing. He just preferred to do it away from prying eyes.

He wandered out to the front porch and leaned against one of the new posts. Grateful for the shade as the sun had already turned the temperature up to "bake," he looked out over his land. He'd grown up in town but had always dreamed of owning land, having room so he wasn't knocking elbows with his neighbors. If the house next door had belonged to anyone else besides Julie Davis, he would have left this one to rot and found another place to buy. But the idea of knocking any of his body parts with Julie's had added value to the place, in his opinion. After last night, he knew he'd gotten a bargain. Hell, he would have paid twice the price and promised to cover the rundown house in gold foil.

A dark-green pickup bearing the logo of a local fence company came up the drive. Colin set his Styrofoam cup on the porch railing and hustled down the steps to meet the contractor. The sooner he got the electronic gate installed and a new fence up, the better off he'd be. Paparazzi were like cockroaches. If you saw one out in the daylight, you could bet there were a hundred more you didn't see.

CHAPTER EIGHTEEN

Colin waved goodbye to the fence contractor then went inside to see if anyone had any questions for him. After clarifying that, yes, he wanted the crown molding replaced in all the bedrooms, he grabbed his bag of dirty laundry and headed into town. Expecting Becky to be at work, he was surprised to see her car in the driveway, so he rang the doorbell instead of using the key she'd given him—in case he changed his mind about the tent situation.

His sister came to the door wearing the same ratty bathrobe he remembered from her high school days and looking a little green around the gills. He retreated to a safer distance. "Whoa. Sorry. If you're sick. I'll go to Mom's to do my laundry."

Becky held the door open wider. "Come on in. I'm not contagious."

Colin held his ground. "Beg pardon, but are you sure?"

She gave him what he called the stink eye and said, "Last time I heard, pregnancy wasn't contagious."

The comment rocked him back on his heels. It took him a second to recover then he dropped his dirty laundry on the porch and grabbed his sister in a bear hug and swung her around, whooping and hollering as he did so.

"Put me down," she yelled, pummeling his shoulders with her fists like she used to do when they were kids, and he swung her until she nearly puked. She was his big sister in age only. In every other way, he was bigger than her, and had been most of his life.

Colin relented, settling her feet firmly on the hardwood floor. "Best news I've had all day. Hell, all week. All month!" he proclaimed. He grabbed his bag of laundry, dragged it inside, and shut the door. "Does Mom know?"

"No. Just you, me, and Ford, for now, so don't you go blabbing it around town."

Colin's eyebrows met in the center as he glared at his sister. "You weren't going to tell me, were you?"

Becky sat on one end of the sofa and brought her knees up under her. Colin took the chair opposite and waited for her answer. "No," she finally said. "I wasn't going to tell you. Not yet."

"Why the hell not? And why haven't you told Mom?"

Becky's tired gaze met his. "I wasn't going to tell you because you ran to Mom with every secret I ever told you."

"I did not." Damn. He sounded like a toddler caught plucking petals off his mother's rose bushes.

"What about the time I told you not to tell Mom I'd lost my library book?"

Colin opened his mouth to defend himself, but she was right. He'd run straight to their mother with the news.

"And what about the time I told you Roseanne and I were really going to the skating rink instead of watching a movie at her house?"

He was guilty that time, too. "I was a kid, Becks. And you were always so perfect. Tattling on you made me feel like less of a screwup."

"I could go on, but I think I've made my point."

"I'm sorry I was such a horrible little brother, but I'm grown up now. I can keep a secret." He trudged down the hall to the laundry room. As he emptied the bag into the washer and added detergent, he smiled to himself. He was going to be an uncle! He loved kids and would shout the news from the rooftop if he could. His smile turned to a frown. He set the dial on the machine then returned to the living room where his sister was stretched out on the sofa. "Tell me again why I can't say anything?"

Becky looked everywhere but at him. His gut clenched as a horrible thought took root in his brain. "Is there something wrong? Are you sick?" He might have been a lousy little brother, but he loved his sister. "Oh, no!" His heart did a somersault. "Is the baby okay?"

She turned her gaze on him and rolled her eyes. A giant smile broke across her face. "Gotcha!" she said. "You are such a worrier."

"And you are a wretched sister." He pushed her feet to the floor and sat down. "I'm going to tell Mom." Becky's laugh was infectious. The corners of his lips twitched as he refused to laugh at his own gullibility.

"The truth is, we'd rather—*I'd* rather—wait to tell Mom until I'm past this morning sickness phase. You know how she is. She'd be over here all the time. They say misery loves company, but in this case, it isn't true. I'd rather suffer alone."

Colin nodded. She was right. As soon as their mother knew, there'd be no getting rid of her. She could hover with the best of them when one of her kids was sick. "I get it. I'll keep my mouth shut."

Becky thanked him with a slice of a chocolate cake Roseanne—of course, she knew about the baby—had sent over, and the two of them talked about the baby and how the remodel on his house was coming along. At last, his laundry was done. He stuffed everything into the bag and set it beside the front door. "You'll call if you need anything, right?"

"Right," she said. "And you'll do the same?"

"Sure. Are you any good with a hammer?"

His jest brought a big smile to her face. "You are such a brat, Colin Parker."

"But you love me anyway."

"Yes, I guess I do."

After admonishing her to take care of herself and his nephew—he was certain it would be a boy—he took his laundry and left. He made another stop at the grocery store for condoms, beer, and bottled water then headed home. He was passing Julie's place when she pulled out onto the road in the old pickup she used to make deliveries. They waved to each other, and he continued on to his place where a crew was setting fence posts for his new gate.

Seeing the workers reminded him of the man he'd encountered this morning. He'd yet to call his publicist so he could start a damage control campaign. *Better to be proactive than reactive*, he thought. He pulled up Cameron's number on his cell phone and pushed the call button. It went straight to voicemail. Instead of leaving a long message, he asked Nashville's premier publicist to return his call then turned his attention to the man waiting on the porch.

"Randy," he said, extending his hand to his restoration expert. "What brings you out today?"

≈∽

Julie waved at Colin as she pulled out onto the road with this month's delivery for McKenna's Liquor Store safely resting in the bed of her pickup. Where had he been?

Her cheeks grew warm as she considered the possibilities. They'd only had one condom last night. He'd promised to get more today. As the flush on her cheeks spread to the rest of her body, she wondered if perhaps a new truck, one with air-conditioning, might be a wise investment. She'd opted for the old truck because it had character, never once considering its flaws. Windows rolled down on her partially restored vintage transportation, she made the familiar drive practically on autopilot. She'd managed to shut out memories of last night long enough to complete the shipment and prepare the invoice she would leave with the cases, but seeing Colin again, even for such a brief moment, brought them flooding back in.

She'd always been one to daydream. Hazards of growing up with next to nothing, she supposed. As a child, she'd daydreamed about being part of a perfect family with a mom and a dad. Maybe a sister.

Never a brother, though. Boys were a mystery to her, and she'd heard they had cooties. Cooties. No one had ever seen one, could not describe one, but knew, without a doubt, they were bad. Contagious even. Transmitted with a mere touch. Maybe even a look.

She laughed at the memory. Colin Parker didn't have cooties. Cuties. He had cuties. He probably wouldn't appreciate being called cute, but he was. Take the tent thing, for example. It was boyishly cute the way he was living in a tent next to his home while it was under renovation. Crazy, but cute. Restoring the old home—seriously cute.

He also had a cute butt. And a cute smile.

"Face it, Colin. You're cute," she said into the wind buffeting her through the open window.

What wasn't cute was his celebrity status. She knew better than to get involved with someone like him. It couldn't possibly lead to anything good, but last night had been oh so good. Better than good. The best ever.

She didn't have much experience, but she couldn't imagine sex could get much better. How could anyone stand it if it did?

She pulled up to the loading dock at McKenna's, dropped the tailgate then knocked on the door. Mr. McKenna himself appeared, and, in a few minutes time, they'd transferred the cases from her truck to his stockroom.

Julie checked the time on her cell phone. She needed a few things at the grocery store then she had to hurry back to the brewery. The temperature on one of the vats had been fluctuating lately, for no apparent reason. She needed to keep an eye on it and determine if it was something she needed to call a repairman for.

Bidding Mr. McKenna goodbye, she hopped into the cab of her pickup. She could spare ten extra minutes at the store. She'd grab a couple of steaks and some big potatoes to bake. Maybe some fresh salad greens. She and Colin hadn't made any plans, unless you counted his vow to obtain more condoms as plans. If he wasn't coming over again, they wouldn't need the protection, would they?

She'd just pulled into the parking lot when a familiar tune filled the cab. She picked up her cell phone and swiped her finger across the screen to answer the call. "Hi, Mom. What's up?"

They'd always been close, and though they'd both moved far away from their old apartment in Houston, they still talked several times a week. She'd wanted her mom to come live with her, but she was too independent to do so. Julie had established a sizeable trust for her with some of her winnings and purchased a condo in a swanky over-fifty community for her. The woman who had sacrificed so much so her daughter could have a good life enjoyed leisurely days learning to play tennis and golf with her new friends. One thing that hadn't changed about her was her love for those trashy celebrity magazines found in the grocery store checkout lanes. She mostly read the online versions now, on her iPad.

"Are you seeing Colin Parker? Is he as adorable in person as he appears on T.V.?"

"How? Wait. What?"

"It was you in the picture, wasn't it?"

Despite the heat that had built throughout the day, Julie shivered. "What picture?"

"It's in the *National Star*. It sure looks like you. Looks like your house, too."

"My *house*?" She felt like she'd been swept up in a tornado. Spinning, her mind reached out, trying to grasp something solid. Something that made sense.

"You haven't seen it, then?"

"No. You know I don't read those rags."

"They aren't rags." Her mother's familiar protest was something solid. She held on to the ridiculous phrase and willed her brain to sort through the rest.

"My picture is in the *National Star*? Today?" She quickly switched the call to speaker then opened the internet browser. Moments later, she found the website. And stared at the front-page photo. Of herself, on her porch, barely dressed and kissing a half-dressed Colin

Parker. This morning. The photo had been taken a few short hours ago.

"Jennifer?" No matter how many times she reminded her mom she'd changed her name, and the reasons why, she still called Julie by the name she'd given her at birth.

"Mom, I can't talk now." She stared at the photo. "I'll call you later, okay?"

"Okay, but it'll have to be late. It's game night at the clubhouse."

"Fine. Late. Have fun. I love you." Not waiting to hear her mother repeat the words, Julie ended the call.

This was bad. Really, really bad. She scrolled down, searching the accompanying article for her name, and breathed a sigh of relief when she was identified only as Colin Parker's sexy and accommodating neighbor. It wasn't a particularly flattering description, but at least they hadn't mentioned her name or her association with Lucky Lady Brewing Company.

She clicked on the photo so it filled the entire screen. Holy hell. This was bad. Very, very bad. She'd expended too much effort making Jennifer Harris disappear to let some rag newspaper resurrect her. She was Julie Davis now. A small-time brewer. A reclusive sort with no past and few friends. No matter how good the sex was, Colin Parker couldn't be one of those friends.

With trembling hands, she flipped through the contact list on her cell phone. Agent Wilkins had said to call him if she had any concerns. This was more than a concern. Panic hovered on the edge of her nerves, threatening her ability to reason. If anyone could accurately assess the threat the photo posed to her new life, it would be the FBI agent in charge of her case.

"Agent Wilkins." Even though she hadn't heard his voice in over a year, hearing it now was like balm on an open wound.

"Agent Wilkins. It's me, Jennifer Harris."

"Julie!" His use of her new name confirmed his continued interest in solving her case. "How are you?"

"Not good. That's why I'm calling. The *National Star* has a picture of me on their website."

The sound of keys clicking on a keyboard assured her he was bringing the site up as they spoke. There was a pause then he asked, "How did they get it?"

She kept the explanation short, explaining she'd had no idea there was anyone around besides her and Colin Parker. "How worried should I be?"

"There are several things you have going for you. They didn't identify you, so your new identity is still intact, and unless your kidnapper reads the *National Star*, he'll never see the photo. When was this taken?"

"This morning. My mom saw it and called to let me know."

"I'll make some phone calls. See if I can get it taken down, but if someone has already downloaded it to their computer, we might be too late."

A chill raced down her spine. "Meaning, it could show up somewhere else."

"Exactly. We simply don't have the resources to troll the internet, looking for one photo. It could pop up on a fan's social media account or a blogger could pick it up. I'll see what I can do, but don't be surprised if it shows up again. Colin Parker is news, especially in the country music world."

"What can I do?"

"Stay as far away from him as possible, and call me if you see the photo anywhere else."

Deep down, she'd known she couldn't have a relationship with Colin, but hearing Agent Wilkins confirm her belief made her heart ache. Would she be alone for the rest of her life?

"I will. I promise. And thanks."

"You deserve to have a life, Julie. I told you we would find him, and we will. In the meantime, keep your head down and your eyes open."

Ending the call, she folded her arms on the steering wheel and rested her forehead on top. She had more money than she could spend in several lifetimes, but the only things she wanted were the things it couldn't buy.

CHAPTER NINETEEN

At the sound of a door slamming, Colin looked up from his latest project—assembling his new gas grill—to see Julie striding across her lawn. Even from this distance, he could tell she was pissed. He ran a quick mental checklist, searching for what he could have done and came up empty. He'd only seen her once since leaving her house in the wee hours of the morning. She'd waved at him in passing—like normal people do. So, what had crawled up her butt and put that look on her face?

Straightening, he placed his crescent wrench on top of the unintelligible instruction sheet and hustled over to the fence where she'd come to a complete stop. When she wouldn't cross the line into his yard, he knew her attitude had something to do with him. He just couldn't imagine what.

"Hey, neighbor," he said. "What's up?"

"What's up? Seriously?" Her expression radiated anger, but her body language was pure defensive. Arms crossed in front of her, shoulders hunched, she was braced for an argument. "You are bad news, Colin Parker. I knew it from the beginning, but I ignored my instincts. It was my mistake. I won't make it again. Stay away from me."

She was halfway to her house when his mouth caught up with his brain. "Wait! What's this about? What did I do?"

Julie stopped and turned to him. The pain he saw on her face slashed him to the core. Leaping over the fence, he caught up to her moments before she reached her porch. "Julie. Wait. Whatever this is, we can fix it. Just tell me what happened? Was it something I did?"

"You can't fix this. No one can."

"I don't believe you. There isn't anything that can't be fixed." Except his broken heart. He could feel it cracking with every word she spoke in that final, fatalistic tone. What he'd thought was infatuation he now knew was so much more. He was in love with her. Had been since their first kiss. "Give me a chance. Please."

Her hand was on the handle of the storm door. Two more steps and there would be a physical barrier between them in addition to the invisible force field she'd put up. It was time to lay it all on the line.

"Julie. Stop. Give me a second." To keep from grabbing the door and yanking it out of her hand, he took a step back.

She took another step then turned. Framed by the edge of the door and the doorjamb, she looked fragile. Broken. Just like him. He ran his fingers through his hair, trying to think. If he told her how he felt, would it make a difference? Maybe not, but as the saying went, nothing ventured, nothing gained. "Somehow, I imagined the first time I said these words to a woman being a bit more romantic. Dinner. Candlelight. Dessert. But staying away from you isn't an option." She visibly stiffened. Colin held his hands up, palms out, and took another step toward his yard. "I'm not a stalker."

She moved again, slipping farther away from him, her eyes wide with something. Fear? God, he hoped not.

"I don't know what I did. You have to know I'd never do anything to hurt you." The invisible wall between them was growing ice crystals. It was now or he might never have the chance to tell her. He cleared his throat, forced his gaze up to hers. "I love you."

⌦⌐

His words hit her like a baseball bat to the chest. She tightened her grip on the aluminum door handle and dug the fingernails of her other hand into the wooden doorframe. How many nights since their first kiss had she dreamed of hearing him say those words to her? She should have been ecstatic, what woman wouldn't be? Excruciating pain radiated from her shattered heart as the words she'd refused to even think in regards to Colin Parker died in her throat.

I love you, too. Oh, god, how she loved him. But her past and his future were rivers too wide and mountains too high to cross. Still, she owed him some explanation for her sudden turnabout. Was it possible he hadn't seen the photo? Even if he had, he had no way of knowing the danger it put her in. He couldn't fix her situation. But he could stay away from her.

"Julie?"

God, he was waiting for her to say something. To return the sentiment. She couldn't. If she did, he'd never let her hide from him again. "The *National Star.*"

His eyebrows rose high on his forehead. "The picture? It won't happen again. I promise."

"Keep the reporters away from me. If you love me like you say, then do this one thing for me. It's all I ask."

"I—"

She didn't let him finish. Closing and locking the outer door, she crossed the porch to the inner door and repeated the process. The little house had become her sanctuary. It had given her the sense of security she'd needed so badly but now felt like a leaky sieve, every hole in the porous sides filled with watchful eyes.

Sagging into one of the kitchen chairs, she closed her eyes and willed her breathing to calm. She'd lost so much more than her privacy. She'd lost her heart, too.

After what had happened to her after she won the lottery, she'd come to terms with living alone for the rest of her life. In the deepest recesses of her mind, she'd hoped one day the danger would become something in the distant past, and she would find someone she could trust. She'd never imagined her heart would have ideas of its own—that it would give itself to someone she absolutely couldn't be with.

Life with Colin would be like living in a fishbowl. Unless she hid in an underground bunker, there would be photos of him and her together, and that was unacceptable.

Sometimes, she wished she'd never won the jackpot. If she hadn't, she wouldn't be living this covert life far away from the only family she had. Despite her degree, she might still be tending bar or waiting tables. Honest, but hard work. She might have met someone by now and gotten married.

But her someone wouldn't be Colin Parker, and she couldn't imagine loving another the way she loved him.

ورى

He should have run over the reporter with his truck when he had the chance! Instead, he'd let him walk away, thinking a phone call to his publicist would be all the damage control he'd need.

You're an idiot, Parker. He pulled the article up again on his computer, clicking on the photo of him kissing Julie so it filled the screen. The photographer had captured the exact moment when he'd changed the angle of the kiss, and, for a split second, Julie's face was clearly visible. Even though they hadn't identified her, it was enough for her to tell him to get lost.

Before last night, he might have accepted her decision, but not now. Not when he knew every fantasy he'd had about holding her, making love to her, had been so far off the mark. They'd been excellent fantasies, but nothing compared to the real thing. He'd been with enough women to know what he and Julie had shared last night had been special.

He was hard just thinking about the feel of her skin, so soft and warm—the sounds she made when he touched her in just the right place—the way her body responded to his—the incredible feeling that he'd come home when he was balls deep inside her.

Their connection had been more than physical, and though she hadn't responded in kind when he told her he loved her, he knew she did. She'd said it with her body last night.

So, why had the photo upset her so? He couldn't say he liked having his personal business on the internet, either. All the other photos in the spread had been of him and his temporary living quarters. Sensationalism at its best. Take something no one would give another thought and twist it so it seemed to be more than it was. Ironically, they'd made more of his dilapidated tent than while wearing nothing but dirty jeans, he'd been kissing his next-door neighbor at a suspiciously early hour. Given the carefree bachelor lifestyle he'd lived in Nashville, he guessed they figured it was par for the course for him. Living in a patched-together tent—that was something they could twist until it fit their narrative.

One thing was for sure. He had no intention of letting one photo keep them apart.

୫୨ୟ

It had been several weeks since she'd confronted Colin about the photo of them kissing on her porch after a night of what she had to admit was spectacular sex. Since then, she'd managed to stay on her side of the fence. She'd rarely peeked out any windows, and she'd worn the noise-cancelling headphones he'd given her to drown out the music coming from his yard every Sunday night. She still took Bud out and walked to and from the brewery building several times a day. It was hard not to notice things. Like, he'd taken down the tent. The lights she'd seen on inside the still-under-construction house told her he'd moved indoors.

His Sunday evening gathering had grown into a full-on event a dead person couldn't miss. Once, when she'd gone out to buy groceries, she'd noticed a teenage boy with a cooler and a lawn chair, manning Colin's new electronic gate. At least he'd followed through on the gate installation, but a teenager was hardly what she'd call security.

Heading home from a long day inside the brewing building, she let her gaze drift to the large group gathered on the other side of the fence. Unable to believe her eyes, she came to a complete stop. Sitting in the spot vacated by the eyesore tent was a shed on a trailer. Had he bought a storage shed and it hadn't been unloaded from the trailer yet? As she watched, a couple of people approached, going around to the opposite side. Only then did she notice the metal stairs visible beneath the raised trailer bed.

"Oh, no. He didn't." She moved closer, her gaze focusing in on the small sign discreetly placed on the back wall of the shed. *Butte Plains Sanitation Solutions.*

He'd put a portable toilet practically in her yard!

"No. No. Oh, hell no!"

She closed the distance between her and the fence line in a few angry strides, Bud hot on her heels. "Colin Parker!"

About a hundred pairs of eyes turned her way, but there was only one set she was interested in. A sci-fi tractor beam couldn't have zeroed in on her prey faster. In less than a second, their gazes met, sending a shiver of awareness along her spine, making her lady parts tingle, and igniting a rage inside her that burned hotter than the flames rising from his fire pit.

Colin stepped from the crowd, his lips quirked up on one side as he made his way over to her. He looked every bit the successful country artist he was in worn denim, an expensive but understated western shirt, and boots polished to a mirror shine. A white cowboy hat sat atop his head. He'd had his hair trimmed since she'd last seen him, and just the right amount of scruff covered the lower half of his face, giving him a sexy outlaw look she found near impossible to resist. Her dog made no effort to resist. Bud slipped beneath the bottom strand of rusty wire and, tail wagging, ran up to greet their neighbor.

Colin bent to scratch Bud behind both ears before acknowledging her presence. "Julie," he said, tipping the brim of his hat in greeting. "What can I do for you?"

Seriously? He had to ask? "You can get your outhouse out of my backyard. That's what you can do." She mentally congratulated herself for sounding rational when her insides were a mixed-up mess of rage and horny as hell.

Colin glanced briefly at the toilet-on-a-trailer then to her, his smile never wavering. "It appears to be in my yard, not yours. Is there something else I can do for you?"

She could think of a thing or two. In fact, she'd thought of little else the last few weeks, but she'd decided to go cold turkey when it came to Colin Parker. No matter how miserable it made her. It was the right thing to do. It was the *only* thing to do. Her life depended on it.

"Are you kidding me? Take a good look, hotshot. You. Have. An. Outhouse. In. Your. Yard!"

He did as she said, taking a good, long look at the trailer before speaking again. "Yep. I believe you are correct. I have an outhouse in my yard. *My* being the operative word. Honestly, I don't want all these folks traipsing through my house to use my one functional bathroom. So, it's either an outhouse or send them off into the bushes." His smile grew brighter, if it was even possible. "Or, I could send them over to your house."

Julie's eyes narrowed. "Don't. You. Dare."

"See, that's what I thought you'd say. So the outhouse stays." He turned, took two steps toward his guests then spun around. "You're welcome to join us. There's plenty of food." With another tip of his hat, he left her standing on her side of the barbed-wire fence and returned to the party.

Julie watched his rear end, magnificent in jeans, strut across the yard. Only after he was swallowed up by the mass of people gathered under his new pergola did she realize her dog had followed him. She could try calling Bud to come with her, but doing so would only focus attention on her. The dog knew where his food bowl was. He'd make his way there as soon as people stopped feeding and petting him, which she could see was already happening.

With a huff, she turned her back on the party and headed to her previous destination—home. As she stood staring into the refrigerator, trying to decide what she would have for dinner, the smell of grilling meat from next door still in her nostrils, her thoughts turned to the person she couldn't stop thinking about.

Infuriating man. Why couldn't her neighbor be ordinary? Reasonable? Just some average guy who liked to play his guitar? Why did he have to be a star with millions of adoring fans?

Why does he have to live next door to me?

For the first time since she'd settled in Butte Plains, she thought about moving. Colin wasn't going anywhere, obviously. She could live here in a perpetual state of irritation, needing what she couldn't have, dodging him and the media attention he brought with him. Or she could move.

It wasn't her first choice of action. She liked living in Butte Plains. Though she didn't have many friends—a conscious decision on her part—she did have a few.

Julie pulled the ingredients for a grilled ham and cheese sandwich from the refrigerator then took a small frying pan from the bottom cabinet. She buttered the bread, stacked ham and cheese then topped it with another slice of bread. While the sandwich browned on the first side, she helped herself to another of her yet-to-be-named brews. This one was her first attempt at producing a lager. She'd spent countless hours researching methods and familiarizing herself with the brewing process before finally committing to giving it a try. Several months later, she'd finally bottled her first batch.

Twisting off the cap, she brought the bottle to her lips. The cold brew slid down, silky smooth with the slightest hint of a rough edge. "Not bad," she said, realizing after she'd spoken her dog had abandoned her for the evening. She took another sip then flipped the sandwich over to brown the other side. Next door, the music portion of the evening had begun. It seemed everyone who owned a guitar, banjo, or other acoustic instrument brought them along to Colin's shindig. What had begun as a casual get-together had grown beyond recognition.

Which drove her thoughts around to the portable outhouse he'd brought in. Since they lived outside the city limits, there wasn't much she could do about it other than complain to him and hope he got rid of it, but, as he'd pointed out, the alternatives weren't good.

Julie plated her sandwich, added a handful of her favorite brand of potato chips then sat down at the kitchen table to enjoy her meal.

CHAPTER TWENTY

Colin helped Randy Tucker with the tricky transition from one note to the next then picked up the tune again with the guitar he treasured more than just about anything he owned. He'd made it himself in woodshop at Butte Plains High School. The project had spanned his sophomore and junior years—something unheard of before, but he'd convinced the teacher to let him do it instead of making cutting boards and salad bowls, the two most popular woodshop projects.

As he strummed and sang along with the old favorite one of his guests had chosen, he let his thoughts drift. He thought about the woodshop he'd begun work on in the old barn. Once his equipment arrived, he planned to start on a new guitar. Something with inlaid designs on the body. This time, he'd use real opals for the fret markers along the neck instead of plastic replicas.

His brain took the leap from a benign subject to one guaranteed to send his blood pressure spiraling out of control. Damn Julie Davis and her delectable neck. Hell, he ached to taste every inch of her. What was with her, anyway? He wasn't sure if she was his muse or his Kryptonite or a mixture of both. Memories of their one night together fueled his dreams, while the wall she'd built between them brought him to his knees.

He'd had high hopes when he'd heard her call out his name earlier, but those had been quickly dashed by the furious look on her face when he'd gotten close enough to see her clearly. He'd wanted to drag her through the fence and show her how much she meant to him more than he'd wanted his next breath, but her body language had told him he'd probably find his dick wrapped in rusty barbed wire if he tried, so he'd fallen back on sarcasm, and if he recalled correctly, pure arrogance to get through the conversation. *Not your best moments*, he thought as he picked up the rhythm of the next song. Thankfully, it was one he could play in his sleep, so he continued to let his mind drift. Too bad it only drifted one way.

His gaze landed on Bud, Julie's Labrador retriever who had taken up residence next to his chair and gone to sleep. If the dog was still here when everyone left, he'd see it got home safely. And maybe he'd get another chance to talk to Julie. Since the sleazy reporter had trespassed and taken a couple of pictures, he'd had a new fence installed along three sides of his property and a state-of-the-art electronic gate to keep unwanted guests out. So far, it was working. He'd convince her he valued her privacy as much as he did his own. And find out why the hell she was so obsessed about it in the first place. There had to be more than she was telling. If she didn't trust him, they didn't have a chance of making a relationship work. Bud stirred, looking up at him with brown eyes he couldn't resist. Bowing out of the song, he petted the dog's head. Shit, he even loved her dog. What the hell was he going to do?

Colin glanced at the house next door. There was still a light on in the kitchen and another was on upstairs. He stood and signaled the Labrador to follow him.

She answered the door, wearing an oversized T-shirt that hit her mid-thigh. Colin's gaze swept over her from her bare feet to her long blonde hair cascading over her shoulders in soft waves. *Breathe. In. Out. Keep your clammy hands to yourself.*

Shit. He hadn't been this nervous the night he'd shown up to collect Sherry Rigs for their first, and it turned out, only, date. He'd been sixteen when Sherry's mother had met him at the door, wearing a pink silk kimono meant for a much smaller woman. She'd invited him in to wait for her daughter, but his feet had felt like lead weights and he'd opted to stay where he was. He'd often wondered what would have happened if he'd followed her inside. He'd never know. Sherry and her mother had moved a week later. No warning. Just up and left.

Standing on Julie Davis's porch, he knew all the way down to his bone marrow—if she invited him in, he'd follow.

Bud didn't wait for an invitation. Tail wagging, he scooted past his mistress and disappeared around the corner. Julie smiled as the dog breezed past her. "Thanks for bringing him home."

"No problem. I owe you an apology."

She cocked her head to one side, silently questioning.

"Earlier." He shifted his feet. "I was rude. I'm sorry. You have every right to be concerned about the toilet trailer. I'll move it tomorrow. I could put it on the other side of the barn. A few more steps won't kill anybody."

"Thanks. For the apology, and for moving the outhouse. It's just—"

"Uncouth?" He smiled. "I wasn't here when it was delivered. Randy's guys let them leave it there. I just never thought—"

"No harm done," she said, clearly intending to shut the door in his face.

"Julie. Wait." The door stopped its forward motion. "Please?"

She leaned against the doorjamb but kept one hand on the door.

"Can I come in? Just to talk."

For the briefest of seconds, he saw indecision cross her face then she straightened and took a step back. His heart pounded. He tested his feet to make sure they'd move when the time came. Then she opened her mouth. "Not tonight, Colin." And closed the door. The dead bolt sliding into place signaled the end of their short-lived relationship.

When the light above the porch went off, he forced his feet into action. He stopped long enough to pick up his guitar and let his guests know they could stay as long as they liked then he went up to his newly completed master suite. As he stripped and climbed into bed hours earlier than usual, he told himself it was because the next day would be a long and busy one. He wasn't retreating to lick his wounds. But as the hours ticked by, and the music from his yard dwindled and the last car drove out, he gave up on sleep. Reaching for his guitar, he sat in the moonlight. Words and notes came in a slow rush as he poured out his anguish to the night.

～∽∽

He felt like hell and probably looked the part, too. There wasn't a damn thing he could do about it except hope it got better on its own. After pulling an all-nighter writing, he'd downed two cups of coffee and taken a cold shower before the limo he'd hired for the day buzzed the gate. When he'd booked this gig to sing the national anthem at this afternoon's game, he'd envisioned Julie sitting beside him on the way to Dallas. He'd screwed his plan up in royal fashion, so, instead of a beautiful woman accompanying him, he had Ford and Scott.

He wasn't at all surprised when they'd accepted his invite at the butt crack of dawn. What red-blooded American male didn't want to play hooky for a day to see the Texas Mustangs baseball team take on the New York Knights in post-season play? Especially if they could watch the game from the owner's private box? It was just one of the perks that came along with the gig. There would be an interview in the press box with the live commentators and a chance to meet the team in the locker room after the game. Win or lose. The national exposure would be good for his career, if he didn't botch the anthem. The Mustangs' organization provided ample time to rehearse before the stadium opened its gates.

"You look like shit," Ford said as the driver closed the limo door behind him. "Late night?"

"You could say that." Long night would be more accurate, but he really didn't want to get into it with his brother-in-law.

"Becky and I are going to have to make it to your shindig one of these days."

"You know you're welcome. Come early, though, if you want a good seat." He couldn't believe how popular his Sunday night get-together had become. Even before Julie had gone apeshit over the portable toilet, he'd considered building a small amphitheater on the far side of the stock tank. He'd have to look into getting a road built and providing parking and a more permanent bathroom facility, but it might be worth the time and expense. He'd seen firsthand last night how annoying the music could be when you just wanted to be left alone. He couldn't blame Julie for being disgusted with his weekly parties. If he were in her shoes, he'd be pissed, too.

The limo came to a stop, and Scott joined them before the driver could get his seat belt unfastened. Ford and Colin both groaned when they saw the New York Knights shirt he was wearing.

"What?" he asked.

"You know we're sitting in the owner's box, right? The *Mustangs* owner's box?" Ford reached around, yanked a Mustangs cap out of his back pocket, and settled it on his head. "And you call yourself a Texan now," he grumbled at his best friend.

"Hey, I've been a Knights fan all my life. You can't expect me to change my loyalty so quick."

"We damn sure can," Ford said.

Colin tuned out the friendly argument. If it kept Ford from digging deeper on the subject of his lack of sleep, he didn't have a problem with it. Whoever said misery loved company had it all wrong.

"Hey, big shot." A jab to his ribs woke Colin from the first good sleep he'd had in two days.

"What?" He sat up, rubbed his hands over his face then helped himself to a water bottle from the cooler built into the wide armrest. "Are we there yet?"

"Not hardly," Ford said. "We just wanted to know who canceled on you at the last minute. We're grateful for the invite, but it was a little last minute."

He took a long pull on the plastic bottle before answering. "Nobody." It was the truth. He'd never gotten a chance to ask Julie, so she'd never had a chance to cancel on him.

Both men laughed like they knew something he didn't. "I never got around to asking. So, no. No one canceled."

"See," Scott said. "I told you we weren't his first choices."

"Hmm," Ford said. "You have any ideas about who his first choice was?"

"If I had my guess, I'd say it was his sexy next-door neighbor."

"Julie Davis? The Lucky Lady Brewing Company girl?" Ford asked.

"She's not a girl," Colin said before Scott could confirm Ford's statement.

"Oh, see," Scott said. "He's got it bad for her. You did see the photo of them kissing, right?"

"That was her? How do you know?"

"Just shut the fuck up," Colin interrupted again. "I thought about asking Julie, but she guards her privacy like a virgin in a harem guards her purity." He clearly needed more sleep. He'd never meant to say those words. Not to anyone, let alone the two happiest men in Butte Plains. They had their women and thought everyone else needed one, too. Well, he didn't. He'd done just fine without one so far. And hell, if he couldn't have Julie, he didn't want a poor substitute.

"Sorry," Scott said. "But have you ever thought she might have a good reason for flying below the radar? There are a lot of assholes out there. It's hard being a woman, especially a single one."

Colin turned to gaze out the window. Could Scott be right? Was Julie hiding from someone? He hated to think of her watching over her shoulder or that someone had done something to make her so cautious.

Colin finished his water bottle and reached for another one. His movement must have been the signal because Ford and Scott changed the subject back to baseball, arguing about which franchise had the better team, Dallas or New York. At least they were leaving him the fuck alone.

CHAPTER TWENTY-ONE

Julie pulled into the driveway of Roseanne and Scott's newly renovated Victorian just around the corner from The Yellow Rose, Roseanne's very successful bed-and-breakfast. It was hard for Julie to decide, but she thought this house might be more beautiful than the other. The color palate of this one was more to her liking. Yellow was okay, especially for a Victorian home, but this subtler blue-gray, trimmed in at least four complimentary colors ranging from green to purple, made the place look like an elaborate birthday cake. Julie liked cake. Always had. She'd become a big fan of the coconut cake Roseanne served at The Yellow Rose. She sure hoped it was on the menu for today's impromptu get-together.

Roseanne had called bright and early this morning to invite Julie to spend the day with her and Becky. Seemed Colin was slated to sing the national anthem at the Mustangs playoff game this afternoon and had invited them to go along, leaving the women with an unexpected day to themselves. Julie wasn't sure what all was on the docket, but Roseanne had mentioned high tea and pedicures. After spending another Sunday evening alone while a party raged on the other side of her fence, she didn't even have to think before accepting the invitation. Though she hadn't spent much time with either woman, she could use a little company. Maybe some girl talk would help her forget the hurt she'd seen in Colin's eyes when she'd refused to let him in last night.

He'd never understand her reluctance to be in the spotlight. She'd done everything short of plastic surgery to make her former self disappear. She'd changed her name, moved to another part of the state, and bleached her hair blonde. And, she kept in touch with the FBI agent who had been in charge of her kidnapping case. Thanks to him, she'd lived to claim her lottery winnings, but the man who'd abducted her and tried to force her to sign over the winning ticket was still out there somewhere. When it became clear the FBI knew who he was, he'd abandoned his scheme to claim the billion-dollar jackpot for himself. After promising he'd see her again, he'd left her bound and gagged in a derelict building outside of Houston. It had taken nearly forty-eight hours for them to locate her. They'd never found her kidnapper.

Shaking thoughts of those harrowing days when she'd thought she'd never live to spend a single penny of her winnings, she followed the walk to the wide steps leading up to the wraparound porch. With its cheerful hanging baskets and comfortable-looking rocking chairs, it was one of the most inviting places she'd ever seen.

Julie rang the doorbell and waited.

When no one answered, she peered through the side window.

"Hmm." She turned around and her gaze fell on Roseanne's new mom-mobile—a brand-spanking-new minivan with every bell and whistle available. A person's car in their driveway most of the time meant they were home, but it was a short walk, especially via the shortcut through the alley, to the B&B. Roseanne had said she'd be here, but perhaps something had come up and she'd walked over to her place of business.

Julie eyed the arrangement of rocking chairs to her right. She could walk over to The Yellow Rose, or she could make herself comfortable. Becky would be here shortly, too. She looked forward to getting to know the other woman a little better.

Settling into the nearest rocker, she closed her eyes and let the peaceful setting lull her almost to sleep. This was the life, she decided, and began to calculate what it would take to build a sitting porch onto her house. At the sound of glass breaking somewhere in the house, Julie jumped up and pressed her nose to the window. She had to cup her hands around her face in order to see inside, but when she did, she gasped. "Roseanne!"

She dashed for the front door, and when the knob turned easily, she thanked God Butte Plains was still the kind of town where people didn't lock their doors all the time, and rushed inside. "Roseanne!" she yelled, approaching the woman she'd come to call friend. The pregnant woman lay sprawled on the floor between the open-concept kitchen and the living area, the shattered pieces of a teacup and saucer scattered about.

"Oh my God! Oh my God! Roseanne!" Julie shook her friend's shoulder. When she didn't respond, Julie whipped out her cell phone and dialed 9-1-1.

Later, as she paced the waiting area of the local hospital emergency room, waiting for word on her friend's condition, she was so glad she hadn't decided to walk over to The Yellow Rose. Who knew what even a few minutes delay could have meant in terms of the baby and Roseanne's survival?

Roseanne's fiancé and baby daddy, Scott Ramsey, had gone to Dallas with Ford and Colin. The men weren't expected home until late. Julie didn't have Scott's number anyway, so, knowing Becky had needed to go into the office for a few minutes to clear her day, Julie requested the number for Adams Manufacturing from directory assistance then dialed and asked for Becky Adams. The nice lady on the switchboard connected the call to Becky's office. "It's a family emergency," she informed the girl who answered. "I need to speak with Becky immediately. Tell her it's about Roseanne." She prayed her friend's name was enough to get Becky on the phone.

"Julie, what's wrong? Did something happen to Roseanne?"

Julie quickly told Becky what little she knew. "I didn't know how to get in touch with her fiancé, so I called you."

"You did the right thing. Thank you." She promised to inform Scott then assured her she would come straight to the hospital. "I'll be there in ten minutes. Call if you hear anything."

She promised, knowing they'd tell her nothing. She wasn't family, and could barely claim friendship with the woman, though the budding friendship had come to mean a lot to her. When she'd first moved to Butte Plains, she'd craved isolation. Anonymity. But as the months passed with only Bud and the occasional delivery person to talk to, meeting Roseanne had made her feel a part of the community. As long as her kidnapper was still out there, she wouldn't totally give up her reclusive ways, but she missed having friends she could trust.

Roseanne's best friend made a beeline for Julie, wrapping her in her arms. "Oh. My. God. Are you all right?"

"I'm fine. A bit shaken." She hadn't realized the state of her nerves until she'd spoken.

Becky led her to a section of plastic chairs and sat with her. "I can't even imagine what you've been through, but I'm so glad you were there."

"Me, too. When I think what could have happened to her if I hadn't…"

"Don't," Becky said. "Let's not borrow trouble."

Julie agreed. "No. We've got plenty already. I was so scared. Roseanne—"

"Is going to be fine. We have to believe that." Becky held her purse in a white-knuckled grip. "Have you heard anything?"

"Not a thing. I'm not family. I've asked, but they won't tell me anything."

Becky stood. "Let me see what I can find out. Ford has donated so much money to them since his dad died, they named the new heart wing after his father."

A few minutes later, she returned, her face red. "They won't tell me anything, either."

"What about Scott? Will they tell him anything?" Their wedding was weeks away so, technically, Scott wasn't related to Roseanne, either.

"If they don't, he'll tear the place apart when he gets here. He and Ford are on the way home. He did say he'd call her parents on his way here. They're in Florida. He's sending his jet to get them."

"That's good. She'll want to see them." Julie knew she'd want to see her mom under the same circumstances.

"Do you have any idea what happened?"

"I haven't got a clue." She explained how she'd arrived, expecting Roseanne to be waiting for her, but it seemed no one was home. "So, I sat in one of the porch rockers to wait. I'd been sitting there for a few minutes when I heard what sounded like glass breaking. The sound came from inside the house. I didn't think. The door was unlocked so I ran inside." She'd never forget finding her pregnant friend surrounded by broken glass and unconscious on the kitchen floor. "I found her in the kitchen and called 9-1-1."

Becky gripped Julie's hands tight. "I know I've said it before, but thank God you were there. I would have been, but with Ford gone today, there were a few things at the office I needed to take care of before I could leave."

Julie covered Becky's hand with hers. "You couldn't have known, so don't go down that path. I was fortunate not to have anything I had to do today, so I was able to go over a little early."

At the sound of the electric doors swooshing open, they both turned. Scott Ramsey blew in like a tornado, his best friend hot on his heels. Scott's gaze swept the room, landing first on the reception desk then on the two of them. Becky stood, dragging Julie to her feet, too. "Scott."

His long legs made short work of the distance between them. He was a handsome man, no doubt about it, but, today, the only thing anyone would notice about him was the worry etched into his features. "Where is she? Is she all right? The baby?"

"We don't know." Becky clenched her purse in a white-knuckled grip. Ford put his arm around her shoulders, dragging her tight against him. "They won't tell us anything."

"They'll tell me." Turning on his heel, Scott crossed to the reception desk.

They didn't have to strain to hear the conversation. After Scott's initial exchange with the administrator on duty, their voices had risen.

"She's my fiancée. And that's my baby she's carrying. I don't give a rat's ass about your policies. You're going to tell me where she is, and I'm going to go see for myself."

"If you try, I'll call security, sir, and have you escorted off the property."

From where they stood, it was clear Scott was about to explode. Becky slid from Ford's arm. A moment later, she dragged Scott to the far side of the waiting room. "Sit," she told him, indicating one of the hard plastic chairs. "Ford knows people." She gave her husband a pleading look. "See what you can do. Please?"

Much to Julie's relief, Scott sat, but his gaze followed Ford to the reception desk. Julie wished she could hear what was being said, but, this time, the conversation remained civil, their voices low.

"I can't believe this." Scott wrung his hands and both legs bounced. The man was a ticking time bomb.

"I know it's frustrating, but I'm sure we'll have news soon." Becky placed her hand on Scott's arm.

"Not soon enough for me."

"You made good time getting here." Julie tried to distract him from the conversation taking place across the room. "Roseanne will be happy to see you."

"If they ever let me see her."

"They will. Just wait and see."

Ford ended his conversation and headed toward them. Scott sprang to his feet, catching up to his best friend in two long strides. "How is she? Can I see her? The baby?"

Ford's smile was reassuring. "Calm down, buddy. I spoke with her doctor. He said she's going to be fine, and a nurse is coming to get you in a few minutes. Looks like you're going to be a father today."

"What?" Scott's face turned ashen. "The baby is coming? Now?"

"That's what they told me."

A nurse in full surgical scrubs came through the doors leading into the main section of the hospital. "Scott Ramsey?"

"Here! I'm Scott Ramsey."

"Ms. Meadows is being prepped for surgery. Come with me, please." She turned and held the door open for him while Scott remained frozen on the spot.

"You aren't going to be one of those men who faint, are you?" Ford asked.

"No." He took a deep breath and let it out. He squared his shoulders. "Hell, no."

The three of them watched Scott Ramsey step past the nurse, and the door closed behind him. Ford turned around. "Everyone is okay. There are some complications with the pregnancy, and the doctor thinks it's wise to deliver the baby by Cesarean today."

"You're sure Roseanne and the baby are okay?"

"Her doctor said she would be fine."

"What can we do?" Becky asked.

"Sit down and wait?" Ford said. "I don't have a clue how long something like this takes."

"Not long, I wouldn't think," Julie said. "Is there anyone we should call?"

"Yes," Becky said. "I forgot to ask Scott if he got in touch with her parents. Do you know?" she asked Ford.

"He spoke to them right after we left Dallas. He had to send his family's jet from New York, so I don't think they've left Tampa yet."

Becky nodded. "Okay. I'll call and update them on the situation." She turned to Ford. "Can you call Kay at the B&B and let her know she'll have to handle things for a while?"

"What can I do?" Julie asked.

"Can you call my brother? Leave a message if you have to, but I'm sure he'll want an update."

This wasn't the right time to tell Becky the last person she wanted to call was Colin Parker, so she nodded and said, "Sure. Not a problem."

"Perfect." Becky already had her cell phone out, searching her contacts for the Meadows' number in Florida.

CHAPTER TWENTY-TWO

Colin retrieved his vibrating phone from his pocket and read the text message from his neighbor. It sounded like Roseanne and the baby were going to be all right, and, thankfully, Scott had arrived just in time. He never would have forgiven himself if the man had missed the birth of his child or, Heaven forbid, something worse had happened to Roseanne. If Colin nailed the anthem the way he knew he could, there would be another opportunity for Scott and Ford to see a game from the owner's box and meet the team members.

The manager for the pregame activities motioned him forward. Colin slipped the phone into his pocket and took his place at the microphone set up in front of home plate. As the stadium announcer introduced him, he waved at the cheering crowd. These were his people, mostly. There were a few people in the stands who wore Knights colors. Country music wasn't big in New York, but, here in Texas, this close to his hometown, people knew his name.

Because of the delay between when the words left his mouth to the time they came through the speakers lining the stadium, he wore an earpiece that fed the prerecorded music to him. All he had to do was concentrate on what he heard through the earpiece and ignore what he heard coming from the speakers. Not an easy thing to do, but he'd done well in rehearsal. He felt naked without his guitar, but unless you were Jimi Hendrix, you didn't play "The Star-Spangled Banner" on a guitar.

Cameras clicked away. Every step he'd taken since he stepped out of the limo had been recorded. Given the way she'd reacted to the photo the sleaze reporter had taken of her and him together, Julie would have hated this. For once, he was glad he hadn't asked her to come along. Scott's theory about her need for privacy gripped him in the gut. He couldn't think about that now. The countdown began in his ear, and he thrust everything from his mind except remembering the complicated verse.

৵৹

Julie stepped outside to make the call but opted to send Colin a text message instead. Call her a chicken if you wanted, but she'd rather strut around the parking lot naked clucking than hear Colin's voice on the other end of the line. No doubt he'd probably prefer the less personal text as well. Especially after last night.

She'd been a bitch about the portable toilet. And though she'd accepted his apology, she'd been a bitch about that, too. Not waiting for a reply, she returned to see if there was anything else she could do to help. Becky and Ford sat off to one side of the waiting room, their gazes trained on a flat-screen television mounted on the wall. Julie glanced up. Colin Parker waved at the crowd as he walked out onto the field at Mustangs Stadium to sing the national anthem. Julie's heart kicked into overdrive as she stared at the screen.

"Come on," Becky said, her arm circling like a windmill on steroids. "Colin's going to sing the national anthem!"

Becky patted the faded orange seat beside her, and, not seeing any way out, Julie sat. Becky had every reason to be proud of her brother. He'd accomplished a lot for someone his age. And, from what she'd heard, he'd done it all on his own. He played and sang only songs he'd written himself. Nearly every recording artist out there hired songwriters or licensed original work to record. "The Star-Spangled Banner" was probably the first song he'd ever sung on a public stage he hadn't written himself. Clearly, his reasons for not covering other people's work wasn't because he couldn't do it because he nailed the anthem. By the time he'd sung the last notes, Julie was a heartbeat away from jumping up from her seat and pledging allegiance to the flag.

Becky clapped and bounced in her seat. "Good job, Colin," she shouted at the TV. "He did great, didn't he?" She didn't wait for an answer. "I wish I could have been there, but oh"—she calmed—"I wouldn't want to be anywhere but here right now."

"Colin wouldn't want you to be anywhere else," Ford said. "He would have come home with us, but it was too late to cancel out."

Julie didn't want to hear another thing about Colin. "Becky, do you think it would be okay if I went over to Roseanne's house? There was broken glass—I don't want Scott to have to deal with it when he gets home." She'd been too upset to notice, but she suspected there had been food left out, too.

"I hadn't given it a thought. Would you mind?"

"Not at all. I'm going stir-crazy sitting here waiting." And she felt like a third wheel. Becky had Ford to lean on. She had no one.

"Me, too," Becky admitted, "but I can't leave. Not until I know Roseanne and the baby are okay."

Julie stood. "Then I'll go over and clean up. Call me if you hear anything. I can get some things for Roseanne if Scott doesn't want to leave her side."

"I'm sure they'd appreciate it. I'll call you. It shouldn't be much longer."

The EMT's wouldn't let her ride in the ambulance, so her pickup was in the hospital lot. Grateful to have something to do besides wait and listen to Becky go on about her brother, Julie drove across town. Like nearly everyone else in the area, she followed the Mustangs' season. The truck's radio only got a few stations clearly. One of those, thankfully, carried the games. She'd just pulled into Scott and Roseanne's driveway when the game announcers introduced their special guest for the inning—Colin Parker.

Great. Just Great. She'd texted him to avoid hearing his voice and now this. She should turn it off and get on with her business, but the moment he said hello to the announcers, her butt glued itself to the seat. They spoke briefly about the Mustangs' one-run lead and the home run by Jason Holder that had put them in the lead before turning the between-pitches conversation to Colin's rendition of the national anthem and his singing career, tying the whole thing back to his roots growing up in Mustangs' territory and his recent return to the area.

"Is it true you're living in a tent?" one of the announcers asked.

Colin chuckled. "Not anymore." He went on to explain about the house he'd purchased and how it'd needed extensive renovations before he could move in. "I still don't have a working kitchen, but I've got a bedroom and a bathroom now. I'll tell you, though, when those saws and nail guns get going during the day, I almost miss my leaky tent."

Julie smiled at the easy way Colin explained what the tabloid reporter had tried to make sound crazy at the worst, eccentric at best. They talked briefly about how Colin had worked hard to get where he was. He'd told her some of his story the night of his sister's wedding, but she hadn't realized until then how much he'd overcome to get to where he was now.

What would he think of her if he knew she could buy him ten or twenty times over with money she'd done nothing to earn? Another reason to keep her distance from him.

Colin got a plug in for his latest release before the inning ended and they cut to commercial. After removing the key from the ignition, Julie grabbed her purse and went inside. The sooner she got this done, the better. She'd need to go home and let Bud out before she returned to the hospital.

※※

Colin followed the Mustangs' employee assigned to make sure he didn't get lost or swamped by fans. He was glad the interview was over. He hated talking about himself. His publicist, however, was probably doing cartwheels right now. He was constantly telling Colin to be more open about his life. "People relate to that shit," were his exact words. It didn't make him feel any better about answering the questions he considered intrusive. He loved singing, would do it for one person or a stadium full, it made no matter to him. But when it came to discussing his life off stage, he figured it was none of anyone's damn business but his own.

Like the fucking tent story. He'd be answering questions about it for the rest of his life. It wouldn't have even been a story if that damn reporter hadn't published the photo of him kissing Julie. Thank God his publicist had gotten the message across—no questions were to be asked today about the kissing photo. Julie didn't deserve to have her face and name linked to him in a sordid way. There'd been nothing sordid about the night they'd spent together—consenting adults and all—but some people could find a way to make something out of nothing.

Was he guilty of blowing things out of proportion? Making something of one kiss on the hood of a car and one night of the best sex he'd ever had when they had been nothing to Julie? Sitting in the luxury box with a perfect view of home plate, sipping a beer that wasn't anywhere as good as the ones Julie brewed, he couldn't focus on the game. He stood and yelled when everyone else did, but he didn't have a clue what was going on down on the field. Just like in Nashville, he was surrounded by people, but alone.

❧❧

Julie had just finished cleaning up the broken teacup when Becky called. "Becky? How is Roseanne? The baby?"

"She's fine and so is the baby."

"Well, don't keep me hanging. Is it a boy or a girl?"

Becky laughed. "It's a girl!"

"I bet she's beautiful. Do you think the new parents would mind if I came to see her?"

"Mind? Are you kidding? They've been asking where you are! I told them, of course, and they're grateful for your help, but they do want to talk to you."

She couldn't imagine why they'd want to talk to her, except maybe to thank her for being in the right place at the right time. No thanks were necessary. "Tell them I'll be there soon. Is there anything Roseanne needs from home?"

"Funny you should ask. I have a list. Can I text it to you?"

"Sure." She glanced at the food intended for the tea party that didn't happen. Maybe she could package some of it up for the new parents and their guests to share. It would be a real shame to let the coconut cake go to waste. "I'll need a few extra minutes, but I'll be there. Promise."

"Perfect. Thank you again. I don't know what we would do without you."

In her eyes, she hadn't done anything extraordinary, but it felt good to be a part of something so special, even if she was only the errand runner. Friends pitched in wherever they were needed. Though her friendships with Becky and Roseanne were new, they felt solid. And that felt darned good.

CHAPTER TWENTY-THREE

Julie was still smiling when she punched the code into the keypad and the gate at the end of her driveway slid open. She couldn't believe Roseanne and Scott were going to name their precious daughter after her! Julie Rebecca Ramsey. A sweet bundle of joy named after her mother's best friend and the woman who had come to Roseanne's rescue.

Julie wiped a tear away just as something darted across the road, illuminated briefly by her headlights. Heart pounding, she hit the brakes. Bud! What was he doing out? Hands gripping the steering wheel, she quickly scanned what she could see of the property. Nothing seemed out of order except her dog was out running around. He'd been sleeping on the kitchen floor when she'd left. Had she left a door open?

No. Absolutely not. After the picture had surfaced in the *National Star*, she'd taken to locking her doors, even if she was just crossing the yard to the brewing house. No. She'd closed and locked the door when she left, and she didn't have a doggy door. The only way Bud could have gotten out was if someone had let him out. And no one in Butte Plains had a key to her house.

Bud stopped in the glare of her headlights, tail wagging and tongue hanging out. Stupid dog. He never met a stranger. She slid the car into Park and opened her door. One foot on the drive and one still in the car, she called for her pet to come. Bud loped over and jumped in the car, barreling over the console to the passenger seat. Julie closed and locked the door then backed down the driveway and out of the gate. Stopped on the side of the road, she dialed 9-1-1 to report a possible intruder. Assured help was on the way, she placed another call to Agent Wilkins.

و&و

"Is that your place?" the limo driver asked.

Colin jerked awake. The lack of sleep last night, coupled with the busy day, had finally caught up with him on the way home and he'd drifted off to sleep. Sitting on the edge of the seat, he peered out the window. "What the hell?" He couldn't tell if the flashing emergency lights came from his place or Julie's from this distance, but he knew. "Nah. Must be my neighbor's place." If it had been his, someone would have called him.

His gut clenched. What was going on? Scott's words came back to him, "Have you ever thought she might have a good reason for flying below the radar? There are a lot of assholes out there. It's hard being a woman, especially a single one."

Hard on the heels of that thought was Julie's voice telling him to leave her alone—all because of a damn photo in the *National Star*. Had she been right to be angry? Had it put her in danger? Had *he* put her in danger?

Christ! He'd never forgive himself if he had. "Hurry up."

When they finally pulled into his driveway, he got out and punched in the gate code himself rather than give it to the driver. He tipped the driver, tossed the bag of Mustangs gear he'd been given on the porch, and ran around the side of the house.

Julie's place was lit up like a circus. The sight of an ambulance amid about a dozen police cars and several fire trucks nearly brought him to his knees, but the need to know if she was okay gave him the strength he needed to cross the yard and hop the fence. He was halfway to the ambulance when two men in tactical gear, rifles raised, stopped him in his tracks.

"Whoa! Whoa!" he said, raising his arms. "I'm Colin Parker. I live next door. Is Julie okay?"

Another man approached, and while the other two held him at gunpoint, this one searched him. After examining the ID in his wallet, the man asked, "Where were you today?"

"I was in Dallas at the Mustangs game."

"Someone can vouch for you?"

"About forty-thousand in the stands and probably millions who watched on TV. I sang the national anthem."

The new arrival signaled for the other two to point their weapons somewhere else. Colin breathed a sigh of relief as they followed orders. The officer handed him his wallet, and Colin slid it into his pocket. "What's going on? Is Julie okay?"

"She's fine. Can't say as much for the brewery, though. Ms. Davis is over there." The man pointed toward the brewery where Julie stood wrapped in a blanket, watching as uniformed police did whatever the hell they did, and firemen trekked in and out of the door. A tall man in a suit stood next to her. "She could use a friend about now."

He didn't know if he qualified as a friend, but he kept the thought to himself. "Is it okay if I go over there?"

"Be my guest." He stood aside, clearing the way.

Swallowing hard, Colin crossed the yard. Red and blue lights flashed across her pale skin. She looked lost and vulnerable wrapped in a blanket while the air around her was typical Texas late summer— hot and humid. Not wanting to spook her, he angled his approach, hoping she would see him in her peripheral vision. His strategy worked. As he grew closer, she turned her head. Her first expression was alarm but then quickly changed to relief as she recognized him. Fast on its heels was the same hard mask she'd worn when she told him to get lost.

"Julie," he said. When she ignored his arms opened to her and trained her gaze on the commotion taking place, he dropped his hands to his sides. "What the hell happened?"

"Nothing for you to worry about," she said.

He let his gaze sweep the chaos in her yard. "Sure looks like nothing to me."

The big man next to her spoke. "You must be her neighbor—Parker, isn't it?"

"Colin Parker. And you are?"

"Special Agent Garret Wilkins, FBI."

"FBI? What the hell? What's going on?" He turned to his neighbor. "Julie? Why is the FBI involved?"

"It's none of your business, Colin."

"Seriously? My next-door neighbor's house and business were vandalized and the place is crawling with Federal Agents and it's none of my business?"

Still refusing to look at him, Julie pressed her lips in a hard line. Colin turned to Wilkins. "Maybe you can tell me what's going on since Ms. Davis seems to think an army of law enforcement, including the FBI in her yard, is none of my business."

"Someone broke into Ms. Davis's house and the brewery this afternoon. They caused quite a bit of damage. I understand you were out of town today."

"Dallas. I just got home. There were supposed to be people working on my house today. They would have been here until about five."

Wilkins nodded. "I've got people chasing them down now."

"You don't think one of them—"

"We just want to speak with them. Make sure they are who they say they are. Maybe one of them saw something."

"Then you haven't caught the people who did this?"

"No, but we will."

Colin trained his gaze on Julie who hadn't contributed a thing to the conversation. A thought occurred to him, and his heart sank to his toes. "Bud. Where's Bud?"

"He was running loose when Ms. Davis came home," Wilkins said. "She put him in her car. After we cleared the house, we put him inside."

"Thank goodness. He's a good dog."

"Not much of a watch dog," Wilkins said.

Colin agreed. "No, he's not a watch dog." Just then, a firefighter wearing a captain's hat approached.

"Ma'am. We weren't able to stop the evacuation from the vats. Someone took an axe to them. Looks like a total loss."

Julie nodded her understanding. "Thank you for trying."

"Our pleasure, ma'am. We hope you're up and running again soon. We're all big fans of your beer."

"That's nice of you to say, but I don't know—"

"If you need help cleaning up, whatever, give me a call. The name's Singleton. We'd be happy to help."

A single tear tracked down her cheek. Julie wiped it away with her fingers. "Thank you. Your support means a lot."

"No problem. It's time for us to get out of your hair." With a tip of his hard hat, Captain Singleton turned and walked away and began issuing orders to his men.

Slowly, the fire trucks left. Then, one by one, the police cruisers followed until it was just a handful of FBI forensics people and the three of them standing in the yard. "Do you have someplace you can stay tonight?" Wilkins asked.

Julie shook her head. "No place I could take Bud. I'll be okay here."

Colin couldn't believe his ears. "What the hell? You are not staying here tonight." He looked at the FBI agent. "She can stay with me."

For the first time since she'd seen him walking across the yard, she looked right at him. "No."

He tried to rein in his temper. She was being ridiculous. "I only have one bedroom and one bathroom. They're yours tonight. I'll get my cot out of the shed and sleep on it. Bud is welcome, too." He looked at Wilkins. "I don't have much else in the house yet, but the alarm system has been installed."

"Mind if I check it out first?"

"Not at all." He dug out his keys and his phone. "I can disarm the alarm from here." He found the app on his phone, and the outside lights came on at his house. "Good to go. Is it okay if I take Julie in her house to get a few things for her and Bud?"

"Yeah. Tell the agent inside I said it was okay." Wilkins looked at Julie. "You can't stay in your house tonight. This sounds like a good alternative for you and the dog until we catch this guy."

"I'd rather get a hotel room."

"A hotel isn't a good idea. We don't know where…this person is. There aren't many places to stay around here."

Julie nodded as the truth sunk in. "Okay." She glanced at Colin. "Let's go."

CHAPTER TWENTY-FOUR

She might as well have sat out under a tree all night for all the sleep she got in Colin's bed. He'd insisted on changing the sheets, but his scent remained to tease her with things she wanted but couldn't have. Seeing his things in the one bathroom they had to share didn't help. Neither did knowing he slept on the other side of the wall.

Then there were the creaks and moans the old house made. Hers made them, too, but she had grown used to those. Last night, sheer exhaustion had made her drift off to sleep over and over again, only to be awakened by the sound of the house settling. Rationally, she knew what the sounds were, but she lay awake listening anyway, just like she had for months after that rat bastard had kidnapped her.

To say she was dragging this morning was an understatement. On any other weekday, she'd have been up for hours. Other than Bud, who Colin assured he would take care of, she had nothing to get up for today. Her brewery was gone. Destroyed by a lunatic with a grudge. Agent Wilkins had told her not to set foot outside alone until she heard from him. She checked her phone for missed calls or messages. Nothing.

Julie dragged herself out of bed and to the bathroom. After showering and dressing, she went downstairs. The house was quiet today—not a construction worker in sight. That, she knew was her fault, too. They'd probably been told to stay away until the FBI cleared them.

Had her worst nightmare been here all along? Working on Colin's house? The idea made her insides turn to ice.

She found Colin in the kitchen, sitting at a table made from an old door propped up on sawhorses. The scent of fresh coffee hung in the air. Bud's food and water bowls occupied a spot under the window where she assumed Colin's new sink would eventually be. She consciously avoided the window since she knew it overlooked her yard.

"Morning," she said, eyeing the carafe of dark liquid. "Where's Bud?"

"He's sleeping on the front porch. Help yourself." Colin motioned to a stack of Styrofoam cups next to the coffee maker. "My dishes are somewhere—Arkansas, I think, along with everything else I own."

He wasn't in the best of moods this morning, understandable. Her cloud of doom had cast a shadow on his life, too. She poured herself a cup of coffee and joined him on the only other stool in the room. She blew on the hot liquid then took a sip. "Moving truck get lost?"

"Hell if I know. Maybe they're taking the scenic route."

She half smiled at his attempt at levity. "I owe you an explanation."

"I take it this has something to do with the photo in the *National Star*?"

"Yes, but it's not your fault. I blamed you, but it was only a matter of time before he found me. Who knows if he saw the photo or not? Crazy people are resourceful."

"Christ, Julie, what are you tangled up in? The freakin' FBI is involved!"

She straightened her spine. "I'm not a criminal."

"What, then? An informant? A witness?"

She shook her head. "Those would fall under the U.S. Marshall's Service. I'm a victim. Agent Wilkins is in charge of my case. My *unsolved* case."

"Fuck, Julie." Colin ran both hands through his hair. "I'm sorry."

She sipped at her cooling coffee before continuing. "Do you remember a couple of years ago—there was a huge lottery jackpot? One person won over a billion dollars?"

"Yeah. It made the national news. There was a follow-up story a few months later when the jackpot was claimed by a corporation."

"Lucky Lady, Incorporated."

"Jesus! That was you?"

Julie nodded.

Colin's brows knit together. "What was last night all about? Is someone trying to get your money?"

"Not any more. Now, he's just trying to kill me."

CHAPTER TWENTY-FIVE

"So," she wrapped up her story, "I legally changed my name, incorporated as Lucky Lady, and moved to Butte Plains. Scruggs never mentioned my mom so I don't think he knew I lived with her. But, to be on the safe side, the corporation bought a condo for her in Houston and I moved here, to Butte Plains. It's been three years. I've become complacent. Put myself out there too much. I don't know how he found me. Maybe it was the photo in the *National Star*. Maybe it was something else."

Colin stood and paced the empty room. "I don't know what to say, Julie." He stopped and looked at her. "Julie isn't your real name."

"It's my legal name. Mom still calls me Jennifer. I don't think she'll ever get used to the new name."

"Jennifer," Colin tried it out. "Would you rather I called you by your real name?"

"No. Too many people knew Jen Harris won the lottery and want a piece of it. The mentality seems to be that I didn't do anything to earn it; therefore, everyone I've ever said hello to in my life is entitled to some of it. I'm sure Ford and Scott have met the same kind of people, but they earned their money." She shrugged. "It's different. So, I'll stick with Julie Davis from now on. Only a handful of people know she's rich."

"So, you're what, a billionaire?"

"I wasn't at first. By the time Uncle Sam got his share, the payout was well under a billion. Thanks to some really good investments, I'm worth over a billion now."

Colin whistled low. "I never would have guessed. You don't act like you have a lot of money."

"Thanks. I try not to. After a few initial purchases—a condo for Mom in a retirement community and the land and brewing equipment—I've hardly touched it for myself. Most of the principle is tied up in investments—stocks, real estate and such. I give myself a living allowance out of the interest then the rest gets rolled over into the investment accounts. And, I give a lot to charity. The new gazebo in town square? That was me. The improvements to the youth facility? Me. I could go on. The list is long. After what happened to Roseanne, I'm thinking about making a donation to the hospital. The maternity wing, to be specific."

He stared. He couldn't help it. She looked like the girl next door, but she wasn't the same person he'd thought she was. "Your charity is admirable," he said for lack of something else to say. He gave to charity, too, but he'd never be able to match what she could do.

"I'm sorry my shit fell on you. If it's any consolation, I'll sell you my property for a reasonable price."

"What? Why would you do that?"

"I can't stay here, Colin."

"Why the hell not? They're going to get the asshole who did this, and when they do, things will return to normal. You can rebuild the brewery. You have friends here."

She shook her head. "You aren't listening. Even if he's caught, nothing will be the same for me. There's something about won money. It makes people crazy. It's as if it's found money, like picking up a twenty-dollar bill on the sidewalk. You were fine before you found it, so you'll be fine when it's gone. All you're going to do is spend it on something frivolous anyway, right? Might as well give some of it to insert name here."

"I don't think that way, and neither does my sister or her husband. And you can't think Roseanne or Scott would care if you have a dime to your name."

"You're missing the point. I feel like there's a target on my back. Sometimes, like right now, I wish I'd never won it. You know what the irony of this whole situation is?"

"No. What?"

"If that bastard only knew how much trouble gobs of money is, he wouldn't have been so eager to get it. It's a hell of a lot of work. Even with an investment broker I trust, there are reports to read and decipher, decisions to be made—constantly." She sighed. "I used to dream about what I'd do if I never had to worry about money again, and here I am, worrying about money all the time. I'm diversified enough, so the failure of one investment won't break me, but that's no reason to be complacent. Maybe I should give it all away—to charity I mean. Life sure would be simpler."

"I sort of understand. I don't have the kind of money you do, but I'm doing okay for myself these days. But along with the money came fame. Like you, I dreamed of what it would be like to reach my goal, now I spend most of my time trying to stay on top. I won't. Fame isn't like money. You can't bank it or invest it for a rainy day. All I can do is hope there are more days of sunshine than there are rainy ones. And keep doing what I do until the rain sets in for good."

"I never wanted fame. Still don't want it."

"What *do* you want?"

"I don't know anymore."

"Meaning you knew once?"

"Yeah." She glanced out the window at her home. "I'd lived my entire life in a ratty apartment building in a questionable part of town. I wanted my own place out in the country. And I wanted to own my own business. Be my own boss for a change."

"You have those things, Julie."

"Had. But even before last night, I'd decided it wasn't enough." She turned to him, her eyes filled with sadness. "I won the lottery, but

I lost all my friends in the process. After the kidnapping, they all knew about the money. Couldn't keep it a secret any longer. Things became awkward. It's the best way I know to describe what had been normal relationships up until then. People who never had a problem talking to me before didn't know what to say, how to act around me. I was the same person they'd known forever, but the money made me different somehow. Suddenly, I was alone, except for the people who wanted something from me—a donation to their favorite charity or foundation. They had no interest in me. If I didn't have money, they never would have spoken to me. And when I told them no, they went away. Then I was really alone.

"I told myself it was okay. I was better off alone. I picked up Bud from a rescue group. He's been my constant and only companion for three years. Bud was enough for a while. Then I met Roseanne and Becky. And you. And I began to think maybe I could have a real life here, with friends and maybe more."

"The kiss," he guessed. "I was a nobody last year. A wannabe country singer."

"You were safe," she confirmed. "Then you came home and you were on top of the world. A celebrity with a huge following and a contingent of paparazzi."

"You should have told me you were hiding out. I would have understood."

"And done what? Locked me away in an ivory tower? I don't want to live like that."

"Do you hear what you're saying? You don't want to live the life of a recluse, but you're afraid to go public. You can't have both. There's got to be a compromise, Julie. Look at Ford and Becky. Or Scott and Roseanne. They've all got scads of money and *they* aren't hiding from life."

"I'm so confused."

"Well, take your time. You're welcome to stay here as long as you want."

"I-I can't—"

"Why the hell not?"

"The forensic team will be out of my house by now. I'll turn on the alarm. I'll be fine."

The idea of her alone in the house while that crazy person was still out there somewhere was wrong. "I'm not letting you stay over there by yourself."

"I'm not staying here."

"Then I'm going with you." Before she could protest, he continued, "I'll stay in your guest room."

Her cell phone rang. She picked it up from the makeshift table and glanced at the caller ID. "It's Agent Wilkins. I have to take this."

Colin nodded then his cell phone chimed. Yanking it from his pocket, he walked into the adjacent room to take the call from Randy Tucker. "Hey. What's up?"

"Sorry about the delay today, but there's good news."

"I could use some about now."

Randy laughed. "I bet you could. Everything quiet next door?" When the restoration expert had called earlier to find out why the FBI wanted to interview him and all the people he had working on Colin's house, Colin had told him about the vandalism next door.

"Looks like everyone finished up and left."

"I'm glad to hear it. Most of my crew has been cleared to return to work today. If it's okay with you, of course."

Colin's gaze swept the unfinished front parlor. "The sooner this place is finished, the better."

"Getting antsy?"

"You could say that."

"Thanks for being patient with me and the crew. We should wrap things up in about two weeks. Maybe less. Oh! And be on the lookout for your kitchen cabinets. They're supposed to be delivered today."

"You mean I'm going to have a kitchen soon?"

"End of the week. Promise."

"Sounds good." He didn't cook much, but he was tired of eating takeout and keeping beer and lunchmeat in a cooler.

Colin ambled back to the kitchen where he found Julie standing at the window, coffee cup in hand. "That was Randy. His crew checked out. They're all who they claimed to be."

"I'm glad." She turned and leaned against the wall so she faced him. "Agent Wilkins told me things should return to normal on your side of the fence today."

"I don't think anything has been normal over here since I bought the place, but yeah, I know what he means." Colin found his abandoned coffee cup and topped it off with the last bit in the carafe. "I know it's chaos here, but you really shouldn't be alone until they catch this guy."

"That's what Agent Wilkins said, too." She smiled and shook her head. "Let me clarify. He didn't say your place was chaotic. He thought I shouldn't be alone."

"Did he offer any solutions?"

"He suggested I stay here for a while."

"And you said…?"

"I would glue myself to you for a couple more days, but no more. If they haven't found him by then, I'm going back to my house."

Colin brought the Styrofoam cup to his lips and sipped the hot brew in order to hide his smile. *Thank you, Agent Wilkins.* "I was thinking you might be able to help me some while you're here."

"How?" She held her hands up, palms out. "I don't do construction. End of discussion."

He let her see his smile this time. "I had something else in mind." His gaze swept the room. "My kitchen cabinets are supposed to arrive today. I need appliances. Randy picked out some options for me to choose from, but I haven't had time to go look at them. Would you mind helping me decide?"

She caught her bottom lip with her teeth.

"I won't let you out of my sight. I promise. We'll go straight to the appliance store and come straight home."

"I guess it would be okay. But later, I need to do some work of my own. Do you have Internet access?"

"Yep. I've got Wi-Fi, too. My mom said I could have my dad's old desk. If you're up to it, we can swing by and pick it up on our way home. Then you'll have plenty of space to work."

"Okay, but we need to be careful. Agent Wilkins said he could be anywhere, watching for me."

"I doubt he'll expect you to show up at my mom's house or an appliance store today. But we won't take unnecessary chances. You can wear my cowboy hat and sunglasses. I'll even borrow one of the construction guys' trucks. Can't get much more incognito than that."

CHAPTER TWENTY-SIX

Colin's hat was at least a size too big for her head, but after she'd caught her hair up in a bandana and stuffed it underneath the crown, it stayed in place. Wearing his aviator-style sunglasses and one of his plaid shirts she'd knotted at her waist, she would be difficult for anyone to identify through the tinted glass on the truck they'd borrowed. Still, her heart raced as they drove through the gate and onto the main road.

"Not a soul in sight," Colin said as he navigated the two-lane winding road toward town.

"That's good, I guess."

"All the law enforcement responding last night might have chased him off."

"Maybe, but I don't think he's done. When he ran last time, he expected me to be dead before anyone found me. I don't think he's going to stop until I am dead." She curled her hands into tight fists as the reality of the danger she was in gripped her.

"Or until he's caught." Colin reached across the seat, covering her hand with his. He pried her fingers loose then gave them a squeeze. "He made a mistake coming here. The people of Butte Plains don't put up with people like him."

"He's nuts, Colin. I don't want anyone here to get tangled up with him."

He gave her hand another reassuring squeeze. "Even me?"

She caught herself before the words, *especially not you*, sprung from her mouth. He'd already said he loved her. Letting him think she returned the sentiment, which she did, would only make it worse for both of them when she left. She forced indignation into her voice and said, "Not even you, Colin."

"Well, that's reassuring. For a second there, I thought you didn't care if I lived or died."

"Please. Can we talk about something else?"

"Like what?" He glanced her way. Unable to meet his gaze without breaking down and telling him the truth—she'd give herself up to the maniac trying to kill her if it meant saving his life—she turned and looked out the passenger side window.

"I don't know. Tell me about your new kitchen. How can I help you pick out appliances if I don't know what style the cabinets will be?"

Colin made a turn and headed toward the freeway where most of the warehouse-type stores had sprung up. They drove for a while in silence then he began to tell her about his kitchen. Staring out the window, she caught a few words. *Country. Farmhouse sink. Copper.*

What was she doing? She should rent a car and get as far away from Butte Plains as possible. Staying here, traipsing around town, even in disguise, was putting herself and Colin in danger. Damn. Why had she ever let her guard down in the first place? *Because I felt safe here.* Her new identity had given her a false sense of security. Allowed her to make friends. To get close to people. Too close.

Colin poked her in the arm. "Julie?"

"What?"

"I didn't think you heard me. I asked you what you thought about the copper accents Randy plans to put in the kitchen."

"Oh." Damn. She'd been so lost in her own thoughts she'd missed most of what he'd said. She had two choices. Admit she hadn't been listening, or answer and hope she didn't sound like an idiot. "Well, I like copper accents, so you're probably asking the wrong person."

Colin nodded, seemingly satisfied with her response. "Okay, then. I thought it sounded kinda weird, but if you don't see a problem, I won't say anything."

A few minutes later, she pointed to a nondescript warehouse ahead on the right. "There it is."

Colin steered the truck into the parking lot. "Doesn't look like much." He put the truck in Park and cut off the engine.

"I came here to buy the coolers for the tasting room." Julie opened her own door and hopped out. "Come on. You won't believe this place."

An hour later, they returned to the truck with a receipt for their purchase. "Thanks for coming along." Colin braked and looked both ways before exiting the parking lot. "I probably would have just tossed a coin if you hadn't been here to help me decide."

Julie smiled. "No thanks necessary. You were right. I needed to get out and do something."

"You up for one more stop?"

"Actually, I was thinking maybe you could drop me off at the tasting room while you go to your mom's. I doubt I'd be much help loading furniture anyway."

Colin gave her a sideways look. "I can load the desk myself, but are you sure you want to risk going there?"

"I need to talk to my staff sometime, and the sooner the better, I suppose. If I *were* to rebuild the brewery, which isn't to say I *will* rebuild, it would take months to return to full capacity. I don't see how I can keep the tasting room open. We'll run out of stock long before I can replace what's there."

"Can't this wait until they've caught this guy? He went after the brewery. He might go after the tasting room next."

"All the more reason for me to shut it down now before someone gets hurt."

"You can't tell them over the phone?"

"No. I can't. I hired these people. I need to tell them in person, and they all should be there in the next few minutes to prepare to open for the day. And you've seen the kind of security the place has. There are cameras everywhere. Inside and out."

"Cameras aren't considered protection."

"No, but door locks are. I'll stay in the office where I can monitor all the video feeds while I talk to everyone. If I see anything at all unusual, I'll call 9-1-1."

"You're sure you'll be safe? You won't leave the storage room?"

"Promise."

"Okay, then. I'll drop you off, but I won't be gone long."

"I don't need much time. I just need to speak to them in person. Rip the Band-Aid off."

"I'm sorry you're having to do this."

"Me, too. But I don't have a choice."

Colin insisted on going in with her. As she'd predicted, her manager was already there, preparing to open for the day. Julie made the introductions. "Avery Mitchell, Colin Parker."

"Nice to see you again," Colin said, extending his hand. "As you can see, I found her."

Avery laughed as she shook hands with the country star. "Indeed you did. It's nice to officially make your acquaintance. I can't believe I didn't recognize you. I'm a big fan."

Wasn't everybody, Julie wondered as Colin posed for a selfie with her manager? The man couldn't go anywhere without someone asking for a photo or an autograph. He'd spent most of his time at the appliance store, smiling for cameras while she looked over his choices and made a decision. He was going to have one very nice kitchen. If hers wasn't almost as nice, she'd be jealous.

"Thanks for the selfie." Avery blushed like a schoolgirl.

"My pleasure," Colin said, sounding like he actually meant it. Julie walked him to the door.

"How do you do it?" she asked.

"What?"

"You know. Smile and act like it's no big deal to interrupt your day for a picture."

Colin put his hands on her waist and pulled her in close. It seemed like forever since she'd felt his hands on her, and damn, it felt good. "It's easy. It *is* a big deal. Without fans, my career is nothing but a hobby, and hobbies, by definition, don't pay. It's people like Avery who make it possible for me to have a kick-ass kitchen and other creature comforts I've come to enjoy. Smiling for a couple of pictures is small thanks for what they give me."

"Well, you made Avery's day. Maybe her whole week."

"What about you? I'd like to make your day, too."

"You already have."

His brows knit. "How so?"

"You got me out of the house, out of my funk. Just being here and seeing what I've built makes me want to rebuild the brew house."

"Hearing you say that makes *my* day." He touched his forehead to hers. "I hoped you'd come around. Butte Plains needs you. I need you."

"Do you really?"

"I really, really do." The low timbre of his voice danced over and through her like a static electric charge, putting every cell in her body on alert. "And once this is all over, I'm going to do whatever it takes to make you see you need me, too."

Aware Avery could probably hear, if not see them, she simply nodded to acknowledge his words.

"I've got to go. I'm going to swing by and grab Ford out of the office to help me load Dad's desk. Then I'll come get you. Can you do what you need to do in say, an hour?"

"That should be plenty of time."

He kissed her on the tip of her nose before letting his hands drop from her waist. "I hate leaving you here, but the sooner I get going, the sooner I'll be back."

"I'll be fine. And I'm not alone, so don't worry about me."

CHAPTER TWENTY-SEVEN

Julie locked the door behind Colin, set the alarm then leaned against the door for support. If they found the creep who was trying to kill her, she had no doubt it wouldn't take much on Colin's part to convince her to give a relationship with him a chance. But if the guy disappeared again like he'd done before, it might be years before he resurfaced. In the meantime, staying here put everyone around her in danger. She couldn't let that happen. She'd done nothing but think about her options since they'd left Colin's house. Being her own boss at Lucky Lady Brewing Company had been fun, but she could hire someone to run the brew house just as she'd hired Avery to run the tasting room. She had the means to hire middle management people to bridge the gap between her and her employees. Avery and the others she employed would keep their jobs. Heck, she'd probably need at least two people, maybe three to do everything she did at the brew house.

Where would I go? The idea of leaving Texas was a nonstarter. Houston was out. Her mother lived in Austin. Maybe she could find a place in East Texas. They'd visited an old friend of her mother's in Athens once. It had seemed like a nice place to a ten-year-old at the time.

"Are you okay?"

Avery's concerned voice snapped Julie out of her musings. She pushed away from the door and rolled her stiff shoulders. "I'm fine. Just needed a couple of minutes to get my head on straight."

"Lord, don't I know what you mean?" Avery said with a grin. "Colin Parker is one fine-looking man." Her grin disappeared. She crossed her arms and glared at Julie. "Girlfriend. Why didn't you tell me who he was when he came looking for you?"

"I was surprised you and everyone else in the place hadn't figured it out by then. He wasn't wearing much of a disguise."

"Speaking of disguises—what the heck are you wearing?" Avery hadn't heard about the incident last night or she would have said something. It had been late, but with social media being what it was these days, she couldn't believe the destruction of Lucky Lady Brewing Company's brew house hadn't blown up the Internet.

She pinched at the flannel plaid and knit her brows. "What? This? Haven't you heard flannel is the new silk?"

"Nope. What gives, boss lady?"

Julie sighed. "Let's have a seat in the office and I'll tell you." She waved Avery into the seat in front of the video monitors and took the only other chair in the small space. From her vantage point, she could talk to her manager and see all the video feeds at the same time. She didn't expect Marty Scruggs to show up—he had a history of running when law enforcement got too close—but she wasn't going to take any chances.

"There was an incident at the brew house last night. Someone broke in and destroyed the place. As a precaution, I'm shutting down the tasting room for a few days."

"Wait! What? Run that by me again. Someone destroyed the brew house? Were you there? Are you okay?" Her gaze swept Julie from head to toe then locked on her eyes. "How did I not know this?"

"I'm fine. I wasn't home at the time." She went on, describing her day from the time she'd left to have tea with Becky and Roseanne, to finding her pregnant friend passed out and the hasty trip to the hospital. It seemed like it had been days since she'd paced the ER waiting for news about Roseanne's condition, but it had been less than twenty-four hours. Avery's mouth hung open as Julie related the story of coming home to find Bud running loose and the frantic call she'd made.

"Why'd you call the FBI? Why not just call 9-1-1?"

"That's another story."

"I've got nothing but time." Avery sat back, arms crossed.

Julie filled her in on the sordid story. At this rate, everyone in Butte Plains was going to know who she was before the last jelly donut was sold at Hanson's Bakery. Her cover had been blown all to smithereens.

"So…you're a billionaire." It wasn't a question.

Julie shrugged. She could almost see the wheels turning behind Avery's startled expression.

"Wow." Avery shook her head. "So, you're just going to close up shop and let this asshole get away with this?"

Julie blinked. "What choice do I have? Opening up today or anytime in the near future puts you and everyone who works here in danger. Not to mention our customers."

"Well, bless your heart." Avery patted Julie on the knee. "It's so sweet of you to be concerned, but that's not how we roll in Butte Plains." She stood, squaring her shoulders and sticking her chin in the air. "Do you have a photo of the lowlife who's after you?"

"Um. Yeah, I can get one." Though she'd be happy if she never saw his face again. She scrambled to process what Avery had said. Giving up, she asked, "What do you mean that's not how you roll?" She had a bad feeling about this. A real bad feeling.

"I mean, let the asshole bring it on!" She pulled her cell phone from the pocket of her jeans. "Excuse me," she said, brushing past Julie to get to the door. "I've got to make a few phone calls." She turned and called over her shoulder. "Find his photo for me."

Oookaaay. Avery disappeared into the front room, phone pressed to her ear. Julie didn't know why, but she followed the other woman's order and soon sent a copy of Marty Scruggs' Wanted poster to the office printer. The ink wasn't dry on the black-and-white printout when a knock sounded on the door.

"I'll get it." Avery sailed in, heading for the door. "You got the photo I asked for, hon?"

"Yes." Julie stared at the face of the man she'd half expected to see everywhere she went since the day he'd left her to die in an abandoned warehouse.

"Good girl!" Avery opened the door to admit half-a-dozen people. In half an hour, what Avery called, The Butte Plains Cavalry, filled the room. Tables were set up and blocks of time spoken for. Copies of the Wanted poster were made and distributed to the hodge-podge group of citizens.

"We're real sorry to hear about your troubles, Ms. Davis," the portly gentleman wearing a three-piece suit said with a smile. "But don't you worry about a thing. You're one of us now. We won't let anything happen to your tasting room."

Julie muttered a thank you as the man wandered off to help the organizational efforts. Avery elbowed her in the side. "See? We're good. That was Harvey Thornberry. He owns the dry cleaners and the laundromat."

Which explained the perfect creases in his slacks. "And the others?"

"Locals." She pointed out a couple of other business owners and a few housewives.

"Friends of yours?"

"Yep. Your friends, too." She'd never seen such an outpouring of support in her life, and it touched her beyond belief. These people answered the call to help a fellow citizen even though they'd never met her. A lump formed in her throat, and she felt the hot burn of tears massing for an assault on her equilibrium. This was exactly the type of community she'd hoped to find in Butte Plains, and her past had shown it to her and taken it away all in the same day.

Life didn't play fair. At least, it hadn't with her.

At the sound of the door opening again, Julie's heart dropped to her toes then rebounded when she recognized Duncan McKenna, owner of McKenna's Liquor. She'd been doing business with him since she'd bottled the first batch of Lucky Lady beer. He'd been one of the first people in town she called friend.

"Julie." He took her in a big bear hug. "Are you okay? I heard what happened at your place last night. Awful. Just awful."

"I'm fine, Mr. McKenna. Thanks for asking."

"The sooner we get this guy off the streets, the sooner you can get Lucky Lady up and running again. My sales have gone through the roof since I started carrying your beer."

She couldn't help but smile at his statement. "I'm glad to hear that." She didn't want to make promises she couldn't keep, but she hated to disappoint the man, too. "I'll do my best to get the brewery back on schedule as soon as possible." And she would, even if it meant hiring someone to run the place for her.

"It's all I can ask." He gave her hand a little squeeze. "Now, if you'll excuse me, I need to see what my assigned time is. Don't worry. If this guy comes around, we'll be ready for him."

She didn't doubt it for a minute. But would Marty Scruggs be stupid enough to make an appearance? He had to know there were FBI agents all over the place looking for him. Not to mention local cops and, now, the Butte Plains Cavalry. He'd have to be really stupid to show his face around town.

The door opened again and in walked Colin Parker. Heads turned. Conversations stopped as everyone gawked at the country star. A heartbeat later, everyone turned back to what they were doing, and the noise level went up again. Colin's gaze found her, and, without preamble, he crossed the room and took her in his arms. "What's going on? Is this the Cavalry?"

"You know about this?"

"Heck, yeah. Everyone in town knows about the Cavalry. I can't believe I didn't think of calling them myself." He shook his head. "I'm an idiot."

"No, you're not."

"I should have thought of this. Who did, by the way?"

"Avery."

"Smart girl."

"I don't know. Is this legal?"

"More or less. We've always had a small police department. The Cavalry has been around for as long as I can remember. They help out with parades and stuff. Rumor has it they used to carry guns. A few of them still do, but only the ones who are volunteer sheriff's deputies. Back in the day, they provided security for a couple of president's who came to town to campaign."

Her gaze swept the assembled group. Julie wondered which ones might be armed. She focused in on one very old lady carrying a purse that looked like it weighed a ton and was big enough to hide a cannon. Lord help her. She forced her gaze away from the pistol-packin' grandma and focused on the conversation. "I can't imagine anyone coming here to campaign, much less a presidential candidate."

Colin raised his eyebrows. "This was a hoppin' place years ago when cotton was king."

"I feel like I'm putting these people in danger." God, she couldn't live with herself if someone got hurt because of her.

"Don't worry. They're well trained. They all go through a training class at the police department once a year. They take their mission seriously."

She could see the truth in Avery's statement. They were a surprisingly well-organized bunch. For the foreseeable future, there would be a small contingent of Cavalry members inside the tasting room during operating hours and more patrolling the surrounding area the rest of the time. She had lost count of how many people had told her not to worry about a thing. "We take care of our own," seemed to be their motto.

"Are you ready to go? I need to get this pickup back to its owner."

"Since this is beyond my control…let me speak to Avery then I'm good to go."

❧

It had taken the better part of an hour to get Julie out the door. Everyone wanted to wish her well and assure her the tasting room was in good hands. Alone at last, Colin asked, "Heard anything from Agent Wilkins?"

"Nothing." The hat he'd loaned her hid most of her expression, but the defeated tone of her voice told him plenty.

"I'm sure they're busy…doing whatever it is they do."

"I know. Agent Wilkins is a good person. He won't stop until he's turned over every rock."

"Have you decided what you're going to do?"

"Yeah. I think."

God, was he going to have to drag it out of her one word at a time? "Care to share with me?"

The brim of the hat caught on the seat, holding the hat in place when she turned her head to look at him. He couldn't help but laugh at the hat sitting crooked on her head. "Ugh!" She yanked the offending Stetson off and settled it in her lap. "This thing is driving me nuts!"

"It makes you look like a kid playing dress-up."

"I'm not a kid, and I'm tired of playing dress-up." She plucked at the old shirt he'd loaned her. "I'm also tired of hiding."

Colin's ears perked up. "What does that mean, exactly?"

"It means, I'm going to sleep in my own house tonight. And tomorrow, I'm going to order new equipment for the brew house."

He hardly dared, but he had to ask. "So…you're staying?"

"For now. One of the Cavalry guys gave me the name of a private security firm. I'm going to call them, see if they can set up patrols around my property and recommend additional security measures I can take. Even if I decide to move, I'd hire someone to run the brewery. After what happened here last night, I couldn't expect an employee to live here without providing the best security possible."

Colin clamped his jaw so tight he wouldn't be surprised if he needed dental work on his molars. She couldn't seriously be thinking about moving. About leaving. He worked his jaw loose and tried to turn the steering wheel to dust with his bare hands instead. "Extra security sounds good." It was the best he could do and not have to apologize later.

"I'll try my best to see they don't impose on your lifestyle." She gave a little laugh and turned to look out the window on her side. "You might want to rethink the fence we talked about."

"Why? Are you trying to tell me something, Julie?" He flexed his numb fingers before wrapping them around the wheel again. "If you are, then just spit it out. I'm a grown man. I can take it." *I think.*

Her next words were spoken deliberately. As if he couldn't catch them all if she delivered them normally. "I'm saying, a wall between our properties would provide you with the privacy you insisted on having."

There had to be something wrong with her hearing. He'd told her he loved her. Not two hours ago, he'd held her in his arms and confessed how much he needed her. "I also said I didn't want a wall. Or a damn privacy fence between us." He enunciated the next words as clearly as he could, considering his jaw hurt like hell from clenching his teeth. "I don't want anything—N.E. thing—between us."

He felt her gaze boring a hole in the side of his head, but he refused to look her way. Refused to apologize for his feelings. He loved her, dammit. What part of *I love you* did she not understand?

"I'm sorry, Colin."

The pain evident behind those three simple words cut through his anger and straight into his heart. *Fuck.* He was being an ass. "What do you have to be sorry about?"

She shrugged. "I don't know. Everything, I guess."

"Everything?" He couldn't believe his ears. Was she lumping him and what they'd shared into her blanket statement? "Even the time we spent together?"

Heat bloomed across her cheeks, and she turned her gaze to her hands clasped tight in her lap. "None of this would have happened if I hadn't let you spend the night."

Christ almighty! "And you're sorry I spent the night?" He peeled one hand off the steering wheel and ran his fingers through his hair in an effort to keep the top of his head from blowing off. "Jesus, Julie. You can be sorry about a lot of things, but not the things we did together. Never that."

When she didn't respond, he silently chastised himself for being an insensitive clod, but dammit all to Hell, she'd enjoyed their lovemaking as much as he had. He pulled off the road, punched in the code to open the gate, and proceeded up his driveway. He backed the bed of the truck up to the front porch, and, before cutting the engine off, he tried one last time to reach her. "I've got a good imagination, Jules, but I didn't imagine the way you responded to me. It was more than just sex for both of us, and you know it. Yes, what happened the next morning was unfortunate, but shit happens. You either shovel it out of the way or get buried by it. You're letting it bury you, and I can't for the life of me understand why you'd rather be buried by shit than be with me."

He slammed the truck door shut with more force than necessary then took the porch steps two at a time. A couple of guys came out of the house to see what was going on, and Colin enlisted their help getting the desk moved into what had been the ladies' parlor but was now going to be his office. When he went outside to move the truck, Julie was gone.

"Well, shit."

CHAPTER TWENTY-EIGHT

Julie slammed the door hard enough to rattle the glasses in the wall cabinet ten feet away. Out of breath from sprinting across two lawns, she clutched the countertop and inhaled deeply. Lord, what a mess she'd made of everything.

She'd spent so much time the last few years lying about...well, everything, she'd apparently lost the ability to speak the truth even if it meant an end to her lonely existence.

What had she been thinking? Apologizing for loving Colin? Because that's exactly what she'd been trying to do. Only he'd seen through her lies—saw the truth eating away at her—and called "bullshit."

Tears spilled over, and she pushed away from the support of the counter. Making it as far as the kitchen table, she collapsed into a chair. Elbows on the table, she propped her aching head in her upturned palms. "Stupid. Stupid. Stupid," she chastised herself.

"I always knew you were a stupid bitch. 'Bout time you figured it out."

Like someone had jolted her with electricity, Julie stood, putting the chair between her and her worst nightmare. Time and life on the run had not been kind to Marty Scruggs. His clothes weren't much more than filthy rags, and, from the odor assaulting her nostrils, it had been some time since he'd showered. His thin hair, once dark, appeared gray beneath layers of dirt. One thing hadn't changed—his crazy-as-fuck eyes. She shivered as the beady orbs scanned over her.

"What do you want, Marty? Do you want money?" Unlike the last time she'd seen him, this time she had access to plenty of money. She'd give him every last dime she had if it meant she'd never have to see him again. "I've got money. Lots of it. It's yours. Just leave me alone."

"You think all I want from you is your money? Money that should have been mine all along?" He took a step toward her. Julie took a step back, realizing too late she'd boxed herself into a corner. There was nowhere for her to go. "You owe me, bitch."

"I-I don't owe you anything." His nostrils flared, and she knew she'd said the wrong thing. Holding one hand up like a stop sign, she said, "Money. I owe you money. Nothing more."

He took another step forward. Julie pressed herself into the corner and gripped the back of her chair. If he came close enough, could she get the chair up and use it as a weapon? She mentally took inventory of her kitchen, inwardly cursing when she realized she'd have to get past Marty to get her hands on anything else she could use as a weapon. *Dammit.* She had no one to blame for her predicament but herself. She'd left the security of Colin's side rather than face the truth.

Colin was right. Their night together had been spectacular. Denying it wouldn't make what they had together go away. Her brain immediately flashed to the day he'd stood on her steps and said he loved her. She'd let her anger and her fears overrule her heart. She should have told Colin she loved him. She should have taken a chance on a life with him. Marty Scruggs probably would have found her. He *would* have. It was clear to her now. One way or another, the beady-eyed nutcase would have found her.

"I'm going to do what I should have done when I had you tied up in that warehouse." Julie watched in horror as he reached behind him and pulled a carving knife from his belt. The light streaming in the window caught the blade, temporarily blinding her. When she raised her hand to shield her eyes, she saw he'd taken another step closer. Panic threatened to overwhelm her, but she wasn't the same person she'd been when he'd snatched her from the gas station all those years ago. Naively thinking she could reason with him, she'd made it easy for him to take her. Whatever he had in mind now, he'd find she wasn't going to meekly go along. Knife or no knife.

"Come out from there, little miss rich girl, or I'm coming in after you." He made a sweeping motion with the knife. "You're gonna take those clothes off, or I'll cut them off. Don't care if I prick you a time or two in the process. I've been dreaming of seeing you bleed for years."

She could see the truth of his statement in his eyes. He'd been content to leave her alone to die a slow death before, but she'd lived. He wouldn't make the same mistake twice. "I'll transfer the money to you. All of it. Just don't hurt me."

"I don't give a shit about the money!" Spit flew as he screamed at her. "You think this is about money, bitch? Well, it's not. It's about you living all high-and-mighty while I've been living under rocks and hiding out. If you'd given me the money then, none of this would be happening now."

"I couldn't give you the money then." She hadn't claimed the jackpot before he'd kidnapped her. She'd signed the ticket and placed it in her mother's safe deposit box while she'd consulted an attorney about the best way to protect herself and her mother once they claimed the prize. Marty had made the mistake of grabbing her on a holiday weekend when the bank had been closed. He'd told her if he couldn't have the money, then she couldn't, either. Then he'd slipped through the hands of the FBI, leaving her to die. "I can now. Let me go. I'll go to the bank and get a cashier's check. Better yet, I've got mobile banking on my phone, I'll do it from here." She whipped her phone out of her back pocket and held it up for him to see.

"I ain't stupid, girl. Rich people like you got money squirreled away everywhere. I bet you don't have enough in your checking account to buy lunch, much less set me up. That's why we're going to do this my way." He held the knife up, letting the light play off the blade. "I'm going to take what I want. What I should have taken when I had the chance. And you're going to give it to me. Right here on the kitchen floor. Hard and fast and you're going to like it, aren't you?"

She was running out of time. She could feel it in her bones. He didn't want money this time, but she'd be damned if she let him have what he did want. As she moved to return the phone to her pocket, she pressed the button on the side five times in rapid succession before slipping the device into place. *Please, God. Don't let the S.O.S. feature be a hoax.*

"Come on out of the corner, missy. Give me what you gave your rhinestone cowboy next door."

At the mention of Colin, her blood ran cold. "I'm not giving you anything."

"Saving it for the man-whore? Word is, he screwed every cunt in Nashville. You were just one more notch in his guitar."

Julie shook her head. "No." She willed her trembling legs to hold her up a little longer. "How? How did you know?"

Marty's yellow-toothed smile made her stomach turn. "Saw you. You think that reporter was the only one spying on his stupid tent."

Good God. The only way he could know she'd begged Colin to fuck her was if he'd been there. Listening outside the tent. Which meant he'd seen their half-naked sprint to her house because their only condom had been in the wallet Colin had left there. Right then and there, Julie made up her mind. If she got out of this alive, she was going to tell Colin how much she loved him, and she didn't give two figs about the paparazzi. Let them take all the pictures they wanted. It was a small price to pay to be with the man she loved.

She focused on the maniac across the room from her. Marty Scruggs might get what he wanted today—but she'd do everything in her power to see he paid dearly for everything he took.

"I ain't gonna say it again, girl. Come out of the corner and take your clothes off. He saw it all. I'm gonna see it, too."

"Come and get it, you bastard. 'Cause I'm not *giving* you anything. You want it, you gotta come and get it."

"Goddamn." He smiled as he approached. "I knew this was gonna be fun."

Julie tensed as he gripped the edge of the table with both hands and yanked it to the side, exposing her pressed into the corner, a pathetic chair in her grasp.

"Maybe your fancy cowboy will still want you when I'm through. Maybe he won't."

Doing her best to ignore the knife he brandished at her, Julie prayed for a chance to make an escape. To get to her, he had to get the chair away from her. Which meant he had to reach for it at some point. He'd expect a struggle. She'd only have one chance. A split second to react.

Wait for it.

Wait for it.

❧❧

Colin checked the Caller ID on his cell phone. Signaling the cabinet delivery guys standing in his kitchen to give him a second, he pressed the receive call button and put the phone to his ear. "Agent Wilkins. What's up?"

"Where's Julie? She's supposed to be with you!"

Guiltily, he glanced out the window at the house next door. "She was, but I guess she'd had enough babysitting. She went over to her place a few minutes ago. Why?"

"Because the 9-1-1 dispatcher just got an S.O.S. from her phone."

Colin's heart stopped. Was she in danger? Had that Scruggs bastard come back? Had she walked in on a trap? If so, it was all his fault. He'd been an ass—again.

Agent Wilkins continued, "When they couldn't make contact, they called me. I'm en route, along with several locals. We need you to open her gate."

Colin nodded.

"You hear me, Parker?"

"I hear you." He was still wrapping his head around the realization he might have pushed Julie into the hands of a man who wanted her dead. She might already be harmed. How long had she been gone? Five minutes? Ten? Hell, he couldn't recall. He'd gone in to get someone to help him unload the desk and when he'd returned to the truck, she'd been gone. Before he'd moved the truck, the delivery van with his kitchen cabinets had rolled up the drive. Shit. She might not be at her house. He could have snatched her right from his yard and taken her anywhere. "I'll get the gate open. But she could be anywhere around here. I'll get my guys to start searching."

"Don't do anything stupid, Parker. This guy is dangerous. He's got nothing to lose, and he knows it. I didn't tell Julie, but he's wanted for a series of rapes across the state. After he left her for dead, he went completely off the rails. We've been one step behind him for years."

"Shit!" He grabbed one of Tucker's men by the sleeve and held on as he ended the call. "Get here, quick. I'm sending someone to open Julie's gate right now." He pocketed his phone and turned to the guy he'd waylaid. "I need you to go open the neighbor's electronic gate. The code is LUCKY. Figure out a way to keep it open. The cops are on the way."

"Cops?"

"Yeah. The guy the FBI questioned you about? He's back. They think he has Julie, and they could be somewhere on the property next door. Go out the front door and stay on the driveway until you're out of sight of both houses then cut across to Julie's driveway. Got it?"

"Yes, sir."

"And keep your eyes open," Colin called after him. "This guy is probably armed!"

The carpenter was hardly through the front door when Colin yelled for everyone else in the house to assemble in the front room. Quickly explaining what he wanted, he admonished them all to be careful as they searched his property. "The cops are on the way. Assist them any way you can."

"Where will you be?" one of the painters asked.

"Next door."

"I'll go with you." Colin's gaze went to the back of the crowd. Randy Tucker stepped forward. "Go, people. Call me if you see anything unusual, but do not engage this guy unless you have no choice."

"You don't have to come with me," Colin said.

"No, I don't. But I think you know something you aren't saying, so I'm not letting you go over there by yourself."

"I saw something in the kitchen window. Like light reflecting off a mirror or something. Julie's in the house. I'm certain of it. I just don't know if she's alone."

"Let's go find out." Tucker headed for the door, Colin on his heels.

They darted around behind several trucks to get to the old barn Colin was using to store construction supplies. Skirting around behind it, they came out some distance from Julie's house. Having been in Julie's kitchen, he knew he could approach from that angle and not be seen from the kitchen window. He pointed out the storm door. "That opens onto the porch/mudroom and laundry room. There's another door inside leading to the kitchen. If we can get onto the porch, we should be able to hear what's going on inside."

"Those old porches are notorious for squeaking floorboards," Tucker said.

"This one is pretty solid. The latch on the storm door might be a problem. As I recall it's pretty tight. Makes some noise when it opens."

"What about the front door?"

"Don't know. Never even seen it."

"Maybe we should give it a try first. We'd have the element of surprise on our side if we could get in that way."

"Good thinking, Tucker. If it's locked, there's always the back door."

"Let's go, then."

"Cops should be here soon," Tucker said as they made their way to Julie's front door.

"Not waiting." Colin put his hand on the old-fashioned door handle and began to press down on the thumb latch.

Tucker put a hand on Colin's wrist, stopping him. "Pull the door toward you to release the pressure on the latch."

Colin nodded his understanding. The house he'd grown up in had the same kind of latch. He'd learned the same trick to minimize the sound, practiced it hundreds of times in his teenage years. With the same patience he'd used to avoid his mother finding out he'd been out all night, he tugged the door tight against the jamb and pressed the thumb latch. It gave with the faintest of sounds. Colin inched the door open enough to see inside.

The door opened onto a small parlor, again, not unlike the house he'd grown up in, only the furniture in this one was new and appeared hardly used. He'd have to be inside to see down the hallway leading to the kitchen. "Clear."

"Careful," Tucker admonished. "Those hinges are old. Who knows when they were last oiled?"

From what he'd seen of Julie's house so far, he knew she'd put some money into it. He'd be surprised if the rarely used front door hinges had escaped her notice. He was betting everything on her having seen to the maintenance of the hinges. Julie had quickly become his everything, so, to be on the safe side, he pushed the door open a fraction of an inch at a time. When he'd created a gap big enough for a grown man to sneak through, he stopped. "I'm going in. Hallway to the kitchen is to the left, behind the door."

"Does she have hardwood floors?"

"Yeah. Why?"

"Take your shoes off. Your socks will make less noise, but you'll have less traction." He shrugged. "It's a tradeoff."

Colin ditched his shoes. Tucker did the same. "I'll be right behind you."

Colin sent up a silent prayer for the help to be on the way but, at the same time, worried the arrival of law enforcement could escalate the situation—if there was a situation inside. He hoped to God Julie was all alone in the kitchen. He could live with scaring the crap out of her as long as she was safe.

They snuck inside and, with Colin leading the way, crept down the hallway toward the kitchen. A man's voice stopped them in their tracks.

"I ain't gonna say it again, girl. Come out of the corner and take your clothes off. He saw it all. I'm gonna see it, too."

"Come and get it, you bastard. 'Cause I'm not *giving* you anything. You want it, you gotta come and get it."

That's my girl! She had to be terrified. Her voice shook, but she wasn't going to give up easily.

"Goddamn. I knew this was gonna be fun." The nasty tone of the man's voice, followed by the sound of furniture scraping on the floor, had Colin moving forward only to be stopped by Tucker's hand on his arm.

"You can't go charging in there," Tucker whispered in his ear. "You getting shot or worse won't do her any good."

"Let me go," Colin snapped as he wrenched his arm free. He dropped his head against the wall and took a deep breath. He was not going to stand by while some lowlife raped and murdered his woman, but Tucker had a point. He couldn't just rush in there. He had no idea what exactly he'd be walking into. A rash move on his part could escalate things beyond all control. He needed a distraction. It suddenly occurred to him there was another way into the kitchen. Signaling Tucker to follow him, he backtracked to the front door. He pointed to a wide staircase. Using a combination of cryptic hand motions and whispers, he laid out his plan. Tucker nodded and gave Colin a thumbs-up to indicate he understood and approved.

Tucker mouthed, "Good luck," right before he snuck out the front door. Moving as fast as he dared, Colin made his way up the stairs, cut across the wide sitting area on the second floor then crept down the rear staircase. Making it to the corner landing where the stairs turned and descended into the kitchen, he paused to listen. Relief swept over him, and his lips lifted on the corners as Julie's curses met his ears. From the sound of it, she was doing a good job of holding the guy off, but how much longer could that last? She was determined, but her options were few.

As if on cue, Tucker banged on the front door then barged into the front room. "Ms. Davis!" he called out, making his presence known.

"In here, Mr. Tucker!" Julie said, her voice quivering.

Taking advantage of the distraction, Colin cleared the final treads and burst into the kitchen. His gaze fell first on Julie. Like a circus lion tamer, she held her would-be attacker at bay with a chair from her kitchen dining set. Scruggs' attention, which had been on the opposite doorway, swung around. Suddenly, Colin was face-to-face with the knife-wielding man.

Scruggs lunged toward him.

Julie screamed, "No!"

Colin jumped back, avoiding the thrust of the blade just as Julie lifted the chair high and brought it down on the assailant's head.

Wood splintered. Blood gushed from a cut on the man's scalp.

Brandishing what was left of the chair, Julie swung again, catching the bastard in the side of the head.

Dazed, Scruggs dropped the knife and grabbed his head with both hands. Like a slow-motion scene, his eyes rolled back in his head and his knees buckled.

Tucker rushed in, nabbed Julie from behind, and pulled her out of the way. Colin swept his foot out, sending the knife out of reach just as Scruggs crumpled to the floor at their feet.

Julie's chest rose and fell with her rapid breathing. Her eyes wide, she glanced over her shoulder at Tucker then at Colin before her gaze landed on Scruggs.

The sound of sirens approaching rapidly seemed to break the spell holding them suspended in time.

Tucker released Julie's arms. "Nice shot," he said. "Remind me never to piss you off!"

Julie reacted like she'd been bitten by a diamondback rattler. Whirling on Tucker, she placed both hands on his chest and shoved. He stumbled against the table and tumbled into one of the remaining chairs. Before either man could react, she turned on Colin.

"What the hell were you two doing?"

Judging from the fury making the veins on her forehead pop out and the cute-as-hell way she was standing, legs wide, fisted hands riding on her hips, he doubted she'd appreciate the only answer that popped into his head—*saving your ass, thank you very much*. He stepped around the heap of sorry excuse for a human being lying on the floor. "What does it look like we were doing?"

"It looked like you were trying to get yourself killed!"

Damn, she was sexy when she was riled up, and she seemed to be riled up almost all the time around him. And if he had his way, he planned to keep her riled up for the next fifty years or so. But first things first. "Would it have mattered to you if I had?"

The first tear he'd seen from her since setting foot inside the kitchen spilled over her eyelid, leaving a damp trail down her cheek. Her lips quivered, and the mask of bravado that had carried her through the last few minutes fell away. Barely a whisper, she said, "You know it would have."

Colin opened his arms. She came to him, pressed her damp cheek against his chest, and wrapped her arms around his waist. Enfolding her in a tight embrace, he thanked God for making her strong and brave when she needed to be and so damn special the rest of the time. Resting his chin on the top of her head, he held her until the approaching sirens stopped and officers swarmed into her small kitchen.

CHAPTER TWENTY-NINE

The sun had set by the time Agent Wilkins wrapped up his investigation and congratulated Julie on a job well done. Through the endless hours of explaining over and over again how she'd come to clobber Scruggs over the head with a kitchen chair, Colin had been by her side. He'd held her hand. Fetched tissues, coffee, water, and snacks. He'd even fed and walked Bud who, oblivious to everything going on, had been living the highlife at Colin's house all day.

Tucker had told his side of the story and left earlier, vowing to check in on her soon.

Julie waved goodbye to her favorite FBI agent as his car disappeared down her driveway. She stood for a moment, face turned to the vast starlit sky, and breathed in freedom. For the first time since she'd won the lottery, she was truly free. Her secret was out, and there were no more monsters lurking in the shadows.

There was, however, one person she'd kept in the dark for too long. She shivered, recalling the moment Colin had burst into her kitchen—unarmed! She'd almost had a heart attack. Yes, he'd frightened her, him and his buddy Tucker, crashing in like bungling idiots, but it had been the realization that with one well-placed jab of Scruggs' knife, she could lose him forever that had scared her out of her wits. When Scruggs had turned on the man she loved with all her heart, she'd done the only thing she could—she'd attacked. And she wasn't going to apologize for it because, in his own way, Colin had been trying to save her. Truth be told, he had. Her arms had about given out on her, and she hadn't known how much longer she was going to be able to keep her predator at bay. Scruggs had had the upper hand, and he'd known it. He'd been waiting for her to weaken then he would have made his move. Up close, she wouldn't have had a snowball's chance in Hades against the knife he'd held.

So yeah, she owed her life to Colin and Tucker. Rubbing her upper arms where they still ached from holding the chair aloft, she sighed into the warm night air. It was time for her to come clean with Colin. Maybe, just maybe, if she apologized for all the mean things she'd said to him, he would forgive her. Then maybe he'd find a way for her to repay the debt she owed him.

He was waiting for her in the kitchen which, she noted, minus one chair and one large knife missing from the block she kept on the counter, looked as if nothing of import had gone on there. Arms crossed, and one hip leaning against the counter, she suspected he'd been watching her through the window above the sink the whole time she'd been outside.

"Figure anything out while you were out there?" he asked.

"I think I saw the big dipper," she said with a shrug. "Or it could have been my imagination."

"You have a good imagination."

She cocked her head to one side. "What makes you think so?"

"I don't know. Maybe it was the way you *imagined* you could hold a maniac off with a *kitchen chair* until help, which might or might not have been coming, got here." He sounded mad, but the way his lips quirked up on one side said otherwise.

She took a step closer. "I didn't imagine anything. I did what I had to do, and I had sent out the S.O.S. on my phone. I didn't imagine that."

"No. You didn't imagine calling for help."

She took another step, closing the distance between them another foot or so. "And I didn't imagine the things I said to you this morning or after you almost got yourself killed by a bat-shit crazy man with a knife."

Colin frowned, his shoulders tensing. "No. You didn't imagine any of those things. You were actually quite eloquent both times."

"I owe you."

This time, it was Colin who cocked his head in inquiry.

Julie continued. "I owe you an apology. I shouldn't have shut you out earlier. I was afraid. I'd been in my self-imposed exile so long, I'd forgotten what it was like to have friends...to have relationships. You were the first person I'd let get close. It scared me."

"Apology accepted."

"And, I shouldn't have yelled at you after. The truth was, my arms were worn out. I don't know how much longer I could have held him off. You saved my life, but all I could think about was he might kill you before I had a chance to tell you I love you."

She said it, and he didn't move a muscle. He just stood there staring at her until her cheeks flushed and she dropped her gaze to the floor.

"That's a nice apology, but as you said, you owe me."

Her gaze snapped to his.

"What do you want from me, Colin? Money?"

"Hell, no! I don't want your money. You can keep every penny. You might have won it, but you earned it. It almost cost you your life. Twice. It's yours to do with as you please. Keep it. Give it away. I don't care."

"What, then? What do you want?"

He stepped forward, closing the gap between them. Toe-to-toe, he reached for her hands, entwined his fingers with hers. "I want the spirited woman who, armed with nothing but a wooden chair, tamed a maniac. I want the woman who survived the unspeakable then went on to build a new life for herself. I want the woman who naps on the bank of the pond with her dog when she should be working. I want the woman who gave herself to me in a leaky tent on a rainy night. I want the woman who built emotional walls to protect herself but found the courage to tear them down.

"I want you, Julie. Just you. I love you. Say you'll marry me."

It would be so much easier to give him the money, but it wasn't what he was asking for. He didn't want anything she *had*, but he did want *everything she was*. She'd spent years guarding both. She loved him. She really did. But was he asking too much? "That's a mighty big price to pay for saving my life, don't you think?"

"It's only fair," he said. "I saved your life. Save mine. Be my wife. I'll even throw in a new chair to replace the broken one. And if I screw up, you can brain me with it."

"Are you going to screw up?"

"And lose the only thing in this world I can't live without?" He shook his head. "Not on your life."

Could she live without him? Her heart two-stepped up into her throat, nearly choking her, and she knew the answer was no. From the first moment she'd laid eyes on him, she'd known he would mean trouble. She'd been right. He said she'd torn down the emotional walls she'd put up, but the truth was, he'd barreled right through them and made a beeline straight to her heart and made it dance.

Mind made up, she pulled her hands out of his and rose onto her toes. She draped her arms over his shoulders, cupping her hands around the nape of his neck. "Okay, cowboy. You throw in a new chair, and we've got a deal."

He wrapped his arms around her, pulling her against his hard body. They fit together like a pair of old boots, and being in his arms felt just as comfortable. "Say it, Julie. Say you'll marry me."

"I'll marry you, Colin Parker. Just say when."

"Tomorrow."

"Tomorrow it is," she said, and sealed the deal with a kiss.

ABOUT THE AUTHOR

USA Today Best-Selling author Roz Lee is the author of two dozen erotic romances. The first, The Lust Boat, was born of an idea acquired while on a Caribbean cruise with her family and soon blossomed into a five book series published by Red Sage. Following her love of baseball, she turned her attention to sexy athletes in tight pants, writing the critically acclaimed Mustangs Baseball series.

Roz has been married to her best friend, and high school sweetheart, for over three decades. Roz and her husband have two grown daughters, one son-in-law, and one grandbaby they couldn't be more proud of.

Even though Roz has lived on both coasts, her heart lies in between, in Texas. A Texan by birth, she can trace her family back to the Republic of Texas. With roots that deep, she says, "You can't ever really leave."

When Roz isn't writing, she's reading, or traipsing around the country on one adventure or another. No trip is too small, no tourist trap too cheesy, and no road unworthy of travel.

Website – www.RozLee.net

OTHER TITLES BY ROZ LEE

Lone Star Honky Tonk Series

Lookin' Good
Hung Up
Rockin' O
Barbed Wire

Mustangs Baseball Series

Inside Heat
Going Deep
Bases Loaded
Switch Hitter
Spring Training
Strike Out
Free Agent
Seasoned Veteran

Lesbian Office Romance Series

A Spanking Good Christmas
Special Delivery Valentine
Pushing the Envelope
Yours, Thankfully

Billionaire Brides Series

The Backdoor Billionaire's Bride
The Yankee Billionaire's Bride

Lothario Series

The Lust Boat
Show Me the Ropes
Love Me Twice
Four of Hearts
Under the Covers

Also:

Suspended Game

Sweet Carolina
Still Taking Chances
Banged on Broadway
The Middlethorpe Chronicles
Hearts on Fire
First Annual BDSM Writers Con Anthology
2015 BDSM Writers Con Anthology
2016 BDSM Writers Con Anthology
Summer Sizzle Anthology

Made in the USA
Columbia, SC
25 June 2018